Death on Edisto

Death on Edisto

Illustrated by the author

Paperback ISBN: 979-8-8229-2062-0
eBook ISBN: 979-8-8229-2063-7

Death on Edisto

Murder on the Island of Misfits

JB King

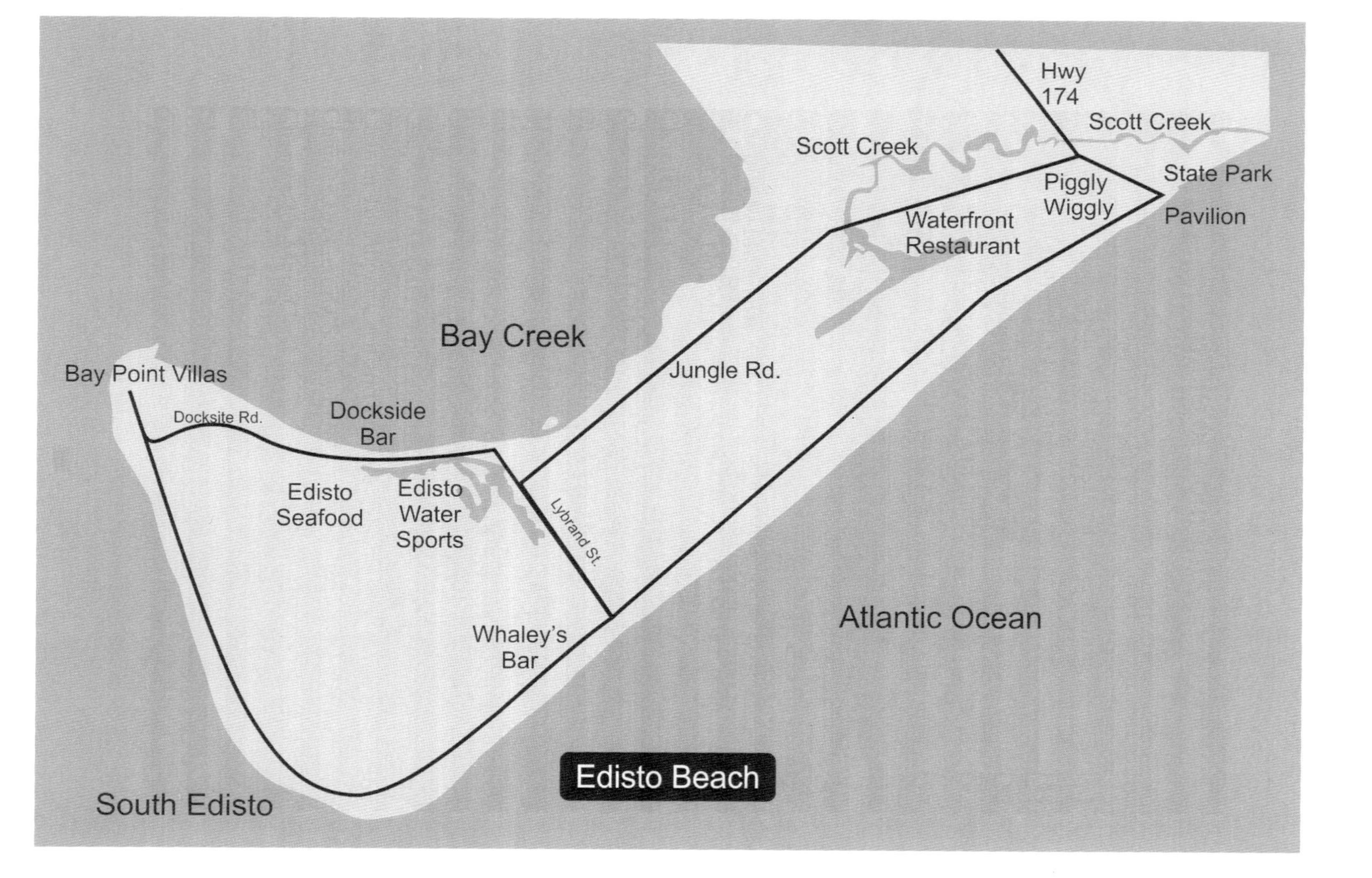
Hwy
174
Scott Creek
Scott Creek
State Park
Pavilion
Piggly
Wiggly
Waterfront
Restaurant
Bay Creek
Jungle Rd.
Bay Point Villas
Docksite Rd.
Dockside
Bar
Edisto
Seafood
Edisto
Water
Sports
Lybrand St.
Whaley's
Bar
Atlantic Ocean
Edisto Beach
South Edisto

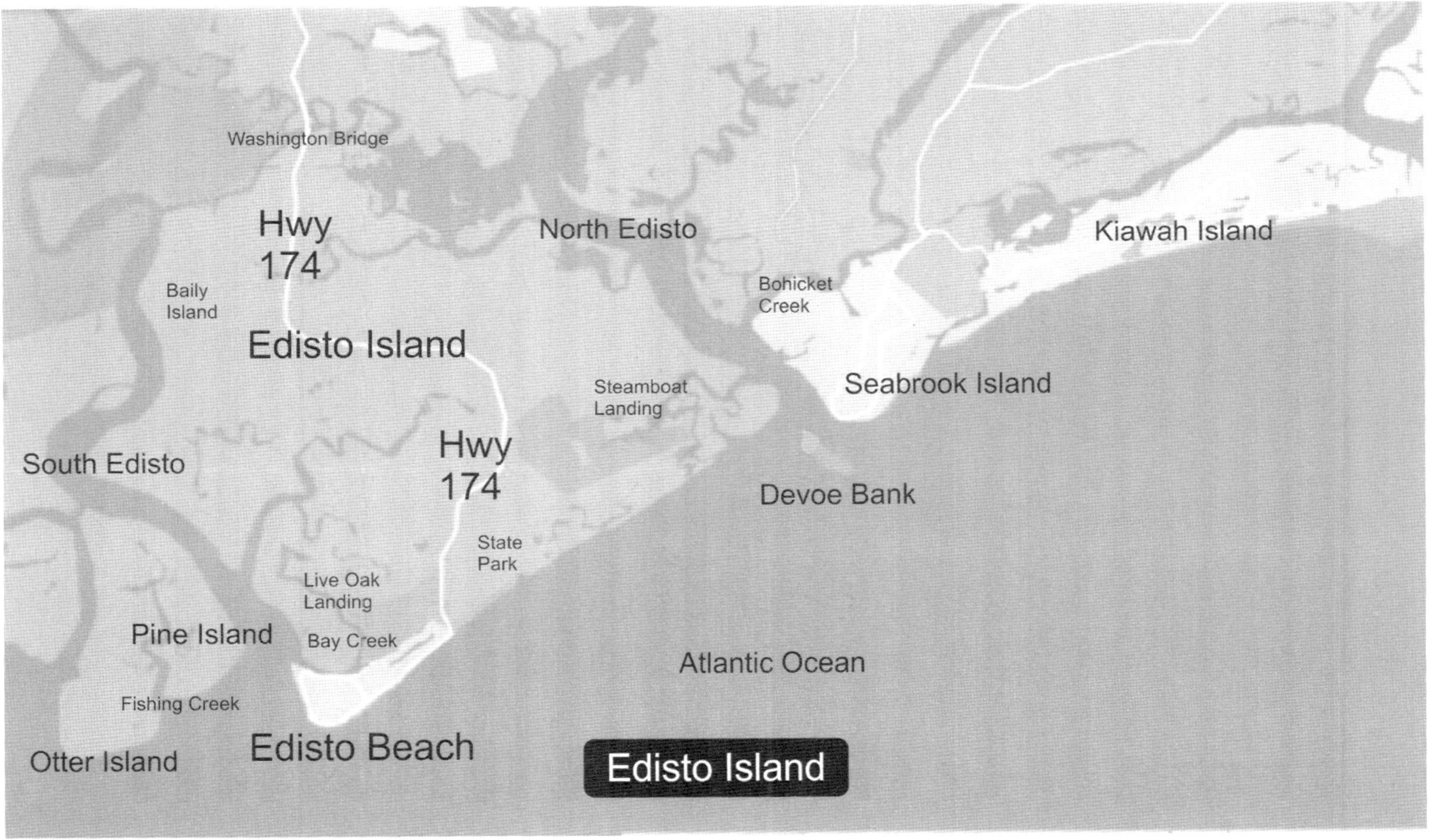

Washington Bridge
Hwy 174
North Edisto
Kiawah Island
Baily Island
Bohicket Creek
Edisto Island
Steamboat Landing
Seabrook Island
Hwy 174
South Edisto
Devoe Bank
State Park
Live Oak Landing
Pine Island
Bay Creek
Atlantic Ocean
Fishing Creek
Edisto Beach
Otter Island
Edisto Island

Table of Contents

This book is in honor of the wonderful people that worked so hard to make Edisto what it was and still hope it will someday return to the old ways.

And a special thanks to the people who inspired this book, and also gave the inspiration to not stop after seeing them every day.

And if you re wondering if it s you I wrote about, I did!

Chapter 1

Discovery

It was a late Monday afternoon in October when Warren walked, or more like stumbled, down the steps of Coots Lounge on the beach side of the Edisto Pavilion and fell into the soft sand. It was the same feeling he had as a kid falling into his grandmother's feather bed. Warren Kaczynski was the local painter and he had a "tooth" for all things alcohol. He was a small man that always looked disheveled, unshaven, and not quite all there. That was just fine with him; he didn't need to impress anyone. For Warren, the days were over when being considered for the Regius chair of modern history at Oxford University in London meant something to him. He was happy with his present life.

Pugzie, his old bulldog, was just as drunk as he was, and it wasn't real clear if he fell down too or just lay down by his old friend. But Warren woke up when the saltwater squirted from the soaked reeds into his half-open eyes as the dog went down.

The reeds always washed up on the beach when there was a real high tide. They call these tides "king" high tides, and this one surely was; it was almost eight feet. On Edisto Beach that meant the rising seawater was about to bring Scott Creek back together again a rare occurrence since Hurricane Gracie washed out the bridge in 1959. The state just pushed up a dike and laid a road across it, creating a causeway, instead of replacing the bridge. This dam stopped the cross flow of the little tidal creek that ran behind the island that was Edisto Beach. Disrupting the tidal flow had taken a toll on the marsh because of the silt and contamination from the houses that never got washed away. The creek was filling in with every tide. Highway 174 was the only way onto Edisto Beach, and when the tide rose too high and covered the road, it would seal off the little four-mile community until the water receded hours later.

But that wasn't Warren's biggest concern right then. No, the single right arm nestled in the water-soaked reeds brought him back to sober real quick. There was no need for DNA testing to determine whom it belonged to. The big Citadel ring and the missing top half of the middle finger were enough to identify the lower part of Cecil LaRoche's right arm. He always used that finger with the missing piece to express his discontent to his fellow Edistonians. He blamed the half-missing digit on a copperhead snake that got him when he was stealing lumber from a construction site on Bailey Island in his younger days.

But where was the rest of him? Cecil LaRoache did have some removable parts, most of his top teeth and his left eye. On occasion, he would take out his glass eye, hand it to his son, and say to the boy, "Go give this to your mom and tell her I'm looking for her." But there was no glass eye, false teeth, or any more of him to be seen that late afternoon.

When Edisto Beach police chief Trent Cappy arrived at the scene, he had all of the lights he bought for his police car flashing. The sirens were blaring and just giving everybody a headache. As he jumped out of the car, the crowd from the Pavilion gift shop, restaurant, and bar, all sixteen of them, stepped back. Trent rushed down the sand dune to the scene of the crime, looked down at the gruesome sight, and promptly ran to the back of the parking lot to throw up. Pale and little shaky, he began to unroll the crime scene tape that he had stashed in the trunk of his car for over six years. Warren walked over and said, "Hey, Trent, let me help you with that tape. You look a little wobbly."

For a career cop, he was not much in the way of a detective (didn't know how to take a legitimate fingerprint; never had to). He had been the police chief at Edisto Beach for over sixteen years, and it was known for having one of the lowest crime rates in South Carolina. That was because there was so little crime, and what there was, he never reported to the state or FBI. He would even hold his hand just above the Bible if he had to be sworn in at court. That way he could fudge the truth if he needed to. Mostly he and his other two officers just wrote the occasional speeding ticket and lots of golf cart tickets.

Golf carts were the dread of Edisto. Every house seemed to have at least one. Even if you rented a house for the weekend, there was usually one or two that came with the rental house. Most renters weren't real good at driving them, and they certainly didn't know the laws.

There was also the Heckler & Koch MP5 machine gun in the trunk of his car that caused a big uproar when he bought five of them and donated them to the town's police force. None of the town's three policemen knew how to shoot a fully automatic weapon, but they were ready if the Russians changed their mind about détente. Trent was just that way, always looking out for the people of Edisto, taking pride in aggravating the hell out of each and every one.

The call had gone out to the Colleton County Sheriff's Department, and they arrived with the necessary tools to begin the investigation. Since it definitely looked like it could be a crime, Cappy called them to assist (do) the investigation. They took a lot of pictures and asked a lot of questions. The women standing around ran to their cars and gussied up a little, just in case one of the pictures made the big national news.

But there were no news trucks or star reporters, just the old guy that occasionally showed up each year in the old Datsun pickup with a camper on the back, standing on the dune watching and listening intently.

Once they were satisfied they had all the evidence they could collect, they took down the police tape and two deputies went to Cecil's office to check for any evidence as to where he might be and to seal it up until the investigators arrived. They quietly and respectfully removed the remains of Cecil, what there was of him that had washed up on the beach. The ambulance, without the arm in it, and the all the other cars headed for Walterboro. Colleton county deputies weren't big on sirens, so they left rather quietly with Cecil's arm in the trunk of the lead car. No need to dirty up the ambulance.

Someone reminded Trent, "Hey, Trent, you better turn off the lights and close the trunk of your car before your battery dies or someone gets your fancy gun." A little frustrated by the comment, he, too, left to go back to Town Hall and write up his report of the incident. The natives milled around the Pavilion for a while, then dispersed in several directions. Most went to Whaley's Store for obligatory informal chatter about the afternoon happenings.

Warren and Pugzie got a ride home with Bobby Hanson, the local Colleton County deputy, who lived on the beach. As they drove back onto Edisto Island, up the causeway of Highway 174, Warren said, "That's a mighty pretty sunset, Mr. Bobby."

To which Deputy Hanson replied, "Yep, I sure hope Cecil's seein' it too."

He was the only police officer that was a full-time resident of Edisto Beach. Bobby was one of the people that made Edisto the type of place everyone wanted to live. He was a part-time preacher and a full-time sheriff's deputy. He always had time to speak to everyone and listened intently as they spoke. And he was everybody's best friend. Everyone wanted him to be the Edisto police chief, but he was happy with his present position. He was also the one person that you would want to deliver the worst news you may ever have to hear. And after he dropped off Warren and Pugzie, he went to do just that.

After unloading the two, Deputy Hanson drove to the LaRoche's home to tell his wife what happened, since he was confident he knew who the owner of the missing arm was. "Always better to get the bad news straight to start with," he reminded himself.

He thoughtfully strolled up the drive to the well-kept house, thinking of what he was going to say and staying inside the whelk seashells that lined the walk way. When Shelby LaRoche answered the knock on the door, she already had Cecil's speech on her lips. But she seemed to melt and turn a little pale when she saw it was Deputy Hanson.

Cecil was known to go missing for a few days, even weeks, but he always turned up with some "cock 'n' bull" story that was totally unbelievable. Once it was the Edisto Indians had kidnapped him, and another time it was a terrible rain storm that tore up his boat and washed him up on Otter Island. But the Indians had moved to Cottageville, about an hour's drive away in the '60s, and Edisto was in the worst drought in six years, and there was still no sign of rain.

Bobby told Shelby what happened and that he was pretty sure it was Cecil's arm. He explained that it didn't mean that he was dead, but that he was in trouble and hurt. Shelby, in turn, didn't know much, but, through her tears, she told Bobby all she knew. Cecil had some business to do and then was "goin' coon huntin" on Oak Island Road for a few days. He didn't mention who he was going with this time, which, upon reflection, Shelby said was unusual. The neighbors and church folk started to arrive, and some of her family must have been called cause they all came in just a wailin'. As Bobby left, he gave Shelby his condolences.

"Now, Miss Shelby, you call me if there's anything I can do for you, and I'll call you if we find anything else." Embarrassed by what he just said, he ducked his head and walked away from the stunned family. He headed for home to write the lesson for next week's Sunday school class. He now had a subject.

Shelby Morton LaRoche, Cecil's wife, was a Southern belle if ever there was one. Prim and proper, she knew instinctively which fork to use, how to sit, and how to place a stamp properly on an envelope. She met Cecil at the Pavilion's pier in their younger years, and they hit it off right away. Her family, the Morton's, had money. Cecil LaRoche had debt, but he had a very a trusting smile. They married two years after they met, and their son George, now six, was the spitting image of his father.

Down at Whaley's Store, Mr. George Timbleston was leaning on the bar from the operator's side taking orders from customers and giving orders to the kitchen as he stirred a customer's drink with his finger. At eighty-three he was the oldest bartender in South Carolina, and many said the grumpiest too.

Whaley's was originally a small convenience store owned and run by Mr. Marion Whaley Sr. He sold gas, bait, cigarettes, and beer. It was the original Edisto Beach local hangout. The Pavilion was more for tourists. When Mr. Whaley died, a group of guys decided they needed a bar for locals and helped to get it open with several tables, some chairs, and an old pool table. Locals were required to bring their own barstool.

Now it looked nothing like it did when they started, and it was hard to tell if it was a bar or a restaurant. The beautiful wooden bar was one of those that are kind a half round one across the back side of the room. Behind it there was a beautiful cabinet built by a local cabinet maker, "Pale" Dale Stall. It held a huge array of liquors and spirits. There were booths in front of the left window of the place and a rudely constructed stage in front of the right one. Tables were strategically placed throughout the room. To the far right were more booths and tables where the tourists and secret lovers usually hung out. In reality, it was not only a nice restaurant but a great Southern bar. The concrete floor and walls were always clean and swept up. And it always smelled like a Southern kitchen because of the okra and fried seafood.

The local men came in almost every afternoon around 4:00 and left usually around 6:00 or just before sundown. No one stayed long enough to get snockered in deference to Chief Cappy. They came to tell the latest jokes and complain about everything under the sun. Yes, the clientele was just like that of any other bar on any other coast around the world—full of colorful, interesting, and somewhat unbelievable characters telling somewhat unbelievable tales.

That afternoon, with all the excitement about Cecil, there was an upswing in business. Many people who were rarely seen in any bar were there to offer opinions and solve the potential crime of the century for Edisto. Sweet William was sashaying through the dining room crowd like a determined man on a mission of universal importance. "Sweet William" Richardson was almost six foot tall and slim or, as he liked to put it, "svelte." He worked as the only lunch time waiter and did it so well; there was no need for another. One of the few residents of Edisto who even knew how to turn on a computer, he was a whiz at waiting tables or defragging your hard drive or even replacing your motherboard. William spoke quickly about the specials of the day and Cecil's right arm.

"What happened to that big Citadel ring he had?"

"It was on his hand. I saw it when they picked up the arm," someone answered.

Everyone had a theory. Ira Woodstone said he knew what happened but was "waiting on the cops to come and ask me. Then I'm gonna tell them everything! Everything about all of you Edisto people!" He was bound to not say what he knew and determined that he wouldn't tell anybody anything, except for the proper authorities. He just kept looking around and repeating himself.

Reecci, the beautiful Puerto Rican cook in the kitchen, poked her head out of the double swinging doors to the kitchen and said, "I saw Cecil hanging out down at the marina a few days ago." She wasn't sure, but she thought it was Thursday when she saw him. "He was talking to three or four people down on the dock, and they sure weren't locals. They were wearing socks and sandals."

Van Mansfield, the present owner of Whaley's, stalked out of the office by the stage and said he hadn't seen him in months. And as far as he was concerned, "I wouldn't care if I ever saw him again. Why, you may ask? Because he's a bum and still has unpaid tabs from last year."

Lowell Richards, the new "manager" of Whaley's Restaurant for the last two months, said, "Not to worry, Boss. Cecil is always good for his tabs at the other bars."

To that comment, Mansfield replied angrily, "Then why are mine over a year old?" He stomped away to check an overflowing sink in the ladies' bathroom and muttered at his new manager, "Dipstick!"

Over at the Piggly Wiggly grocery store, you couldn't get in the front door of the place. The other locals had blocked the automatic entrance door with their buggies while talking, and it was constantly trying to open and close. So many people were commenting on the disappearance of Cecil (well, at least the unfound part of him) that it was getting unnerving.

Julia Horton, who drove the local tow truck, said, "It was bound to come to this. I just knew he was headed down the wrong path. He's been living life on the edge, and it caught up to him."

Helen Pace, the Baptist patriarch of Edisto, said to Julia "You shouldn't talk that way about the dead. There's some good in everyone."

David Walters, the store manager chimed in, "Miss Helen, you're right. It might just take a little time to find that spot of good in Cecil. Anyway, who says he's dead? People can live without an arm." He gently ushered them past his confused door with more nods and smiles.

The only grocery store on Edisto and for about forty miles, the Piggly Wiggly was the center of Edisto life. The residents loved their little store and adored the manager and the assistant manager, Bradley Pitman. Brad, as everyone called him, had a slight resemblance to that other famous Brad, the actor with the slightly shorter last name. All of the ladies loved to see him and would introduce him to their daughters and granddaughters when they came to visit. He was polite and honored to make their acquaintance and always made a bit of a fuss over them.

Walters was another Edisto gem. David helped everyone out when they needed it, no matter who they were. He gave those who couldn't get a job anywhere at least one chance. He donated in spite of corporate rules and guidelines. The big corporate guys would come, spend the day, and go home thankful for having such a good employee representing their company. They left bitten by the "Edisto bug," that little annoying itch that made you think, "If all the world were like Edisto…"

And it went on around town like that for days. Whether it was the U.S. post office (not the smallest around; Adams Run had only one six-by-eight-foot room), the Old Post Office Restaurant (more world renowned than many of the top Charleston restaurants), or the True Value Hardware Store (where if we don't have it, we can get it by tomorrow), everyone was talking about where the rest of Cecil could be and what on earth he could have got himself into.

Chapter 2

The Burial

Over on Pine Island, he buried her again…but this time, a little deeper.

Chapter 3

Plane Drop

The next morning after Cecil's arm was found, a cold front moved in, and there was a heavy fog out over the ocean. A small plane came in low and landed on the seaward side of Otter Island, far out of sight of the populated beaches. It was low tide and the beach was wide and clear. The light wind was perfect, and the foggy mist had kept the visibility low, so no one saw it approach. The Cessna 152 glided silently in with the motor at low throttle and never completely stopping as it touched down. It turned, reversed its direction, and slowed just enough for a hooded sprinter to run out of the coastal forest, throw something in the open door, and jump on the wing brace. The pilot checked quickly to see that there was cash inside and noticed the small knife with a strange downward curved blade. "Bonus," he said aloud and pushed a black backpack out the other door. Then he powered up the engine again, and the plane lifted off the beach and banked into a tight turn.

It flew out low over the ocean toward Beaufort. It was about a minute out and about two miles off shore when it exploded.

It had disappeared quickly in a huge fireball that lasted only seconds. There were far more explosives in the package than were needed for such a small plane. The first small charge dispersed the contents of two flammable gas cylinders and spread six delayed blasting caps hidden underneath the cash. The highly pressurized gas quickly penetrated every crevice of the craft. The caps exploded seconds later, igniting the fuel air mixture into an incredible 2,700 degree fireball. The plane just disappeared into the vacuum of the mushroom cloud that rose skyward. There was no oil slick, only a little smoke and a few small parts that fell across a wide area. What was left sank quickly in the gently rolling waves.

Chapter 4

Sprinter

The hooded sprinter turned away from the fireball, smiled, and began to walk calmly along the beach toward St. Helena Sound with the small but heavy backpack, listening for the sound of other motors. There were none. After the explosion, the wind picked up and the sky began to clear. The hooded sweatshirt was pulled back and exposed a new Ducks Unlimited hat. A pair of classic Wayfarer sunglasses came out of one pocket and a cell phone from another. A quick stop to send a text, and the convertible pants legs were unzipped and came off to make a pair of shorts. More comfortable, he picked up the pace, and the three miles were covered quickly.

At Fenwick Cut the backpack went into the long, sleek boat with a heavy thud. The sprinter vaulted over the gunnel right behind it. The winch hummed, and it locked the bow anchor into place securely. The twin motors started quickly with a deep rumble as the shorts and hood came off even quicker. A long stretch of the arms and legs exposed a hard, tanned body in a black bikini bottom and tight cutoff T-shirt. The hat was thrown under the console, and long black hair was unleashed to the warm salt air. It flowed like a signal flag with grace and wrapped itself around her neck, almost covering the necklace she always wore. As the powerful twenty-five foot Contender motored past the beach at Otter Island, she remembered catching finger mullets and blue crabs in the small creek that flowed from the interior of the island as a child. Her eyes got glassy with tears, but only for a second. She growled at herself for being weak and ripped off her T-shirt, exposing even more of her beauty. She wiped her eyes and nose with it, then threw it into the waves. Ironically, the "Just Say No to Drugs" logo spread wide on the waves.

The Contender was a strong, fast boat that could almost take flight and ride on top of rough water. She then pushed the throttle open and let the twin two-hundred horsepower motors try. She loved the big black boat, and she loved the water, but she hated Edisto.

Chapter 5

Bo McKee Gets the Case

Bo McKee walked into the Colleton County Sheriff's office in Walterboro the next morning. It was the day after the discovery of the severed arm. He held a small paper cup of very hot black coffee. As he blew across the top of it to cool it down, he stopped and looked through the steam gently rising from the cup at the sheriff's assistant, Mary.

Mary Cunningham was not your typical Southern belle. Mary had a bachelor's degree in public relations from Clemson and her master's degree in criminology from the University of South Carolina. And she knew the law like no other in the South Carolina Lowcountry. She fought the "good ol' boy" system every day, and either you loved her for her brains and looks, or you hated her—again, for her looks and brains. There was no place in the middle. Tall, five feet nine in flats, she was stunning. No one knew much about her, except that she came to Walterboro from the area of Boiling Springs, known as the upstate of South Carolina. She had that mild complexion that made you wonder.

Was she a light-skinned Black, Puerto Rican, or Mulatto? Anyway, she could stop a tractor during the height of harvest. Her deep green eyes made the fellows melt and the women pay closer attention to their men. Mary quietly said to Bo without looking up, "Got a big one on Edisto this time, ya know. You can bet he's gonna put you on this case, even if he is still pissed at you about your last arrest."

"Why?" asked the smirking detective.

"You only got a conviction because of that so-called confession.

Bo replied, "It was just my charming personality."

Mary replied a little more sternly, "Not many murders get solved on Edisto. Those uppity beach people keep pretty quiet and to themselves." She immediately blushed and looked away.

Mary was referring to the murders and suspicious deaths that never seemed to get solved on Edisto. It started with old man McConkey getting shot and stabbed one night in the late 1920s. McConkey came to Edisto to plant the long fiber Sea Island cotton, but labor problems and the cotton boll weevil took care of that. So he went into cattle farming and was doing alright with it. He was known to carry large sums of money, letters of credit from the local banks, and a loaded gun. Those letters of credit were just like a blank check—all you had to do was make it payable to yourself, and the bank would give you cold, hard cash. No questions asked.

One night someone apparently got the drop on him and relieved him of all of that cash and notes with their own gun and a knife. They made sure the job was complete. He was shot and cut so bad the only part that wasn't bloody was the bottom of his feet.

Other unsolved crimes included a local man who had supposedly committed suicide by cutting his own throat and throwing the knife out of the window. It had landed up on the second-floor veranda on the far side of the house. He was on the first floor. Then there was the young Black boy seen dancing at the Pavilion with the white women who washed up on the beach a week later. What crimes there were just didn't seem get solved on Edisto, including one that was near and dear to the detective.

Chapter 6

Those From Off

Locals always said that the other people "from off" who moved to Edisto were running from something or hiding from something. Boykin McKee was doing neither. He had come running to Edisto to find something—the man who had kidnapped and murdered his wife Freedia.

Freedia had been abducted leaving Trinity Episcopal Church after helping with the Parkinson's Support Group. Every Friday she would drive down to Edisto from their house in Charleston and help those who couldn't make her Charleston meetings. She would stay at her family's beach house overnight and return home the next day. If he could get off for the weekend, he would drive down also, and they would have a "free weekend," meaning a weekend all alone and to themselves. She held the meetings for two years.

As she drove home to her family's beach house after her meeting one night, she stopped to help what she thought was an older man who had broken down right at the Mystery Tree and Botany Bay Road on highway 174. Several other people that had been at the meeting passed her, and she had waved them off as if everything was alright.

Her mutilated body was found three days later by a game warden. Her beaten and tortured body was hanging from a tree.

The only clues came from what those elderly people saw about sunset—a big, dirty green van with stripes on the sides and an older man with a funny torn hat and a short gray beard. They were all so sorry they could be of such little help. Detective McKee still worked that case every day in his mind.

Chapter 7

Sheriff

Mary, embarrassed about bringing up Freedia's murder, told Bo to go on in without looking up. "He's on the phone with the attorney general; I think he's almost finished."

When he entered Sheriff Jeff Malory's office, he actually was still on the phone with Harry McMaster, the South Carolina attorney general. Malory was Colleton County's first Black sheriff since reconstruction. Smart and no nonsense, he was saddled by the old boy system and the new gangs that were tearing his community apart. He was recruiting help from anyone who would listen, and right now he was working all of the state officials who would take his call.

Bo sat down under the watchful eye of his superior. The office walls were covered with pictures of the sheriff and lots of famous and infamous people: Strom Thurmond, Fritz Hollings, both George Bushes, even Hillary Clinton. And there were the others like Pee Wee Gaskins and Susan Smith, both of whom he helped convict. The building was an old school that the county converted into offices. The windows were six feet high with about thirty small panes of glass in each one. The wall paint was some kind of pale green trimmed in white. He had to hand it to the sheriff; he made the best of it by covering it up with pictures.

He caught the last of the conversation, and it seemed McMaster was also looking for support in the upcoming governor's race. Malory hung up the phone and shook his head. Then he quickly turned his attention to the detective and his coffee. The sheriff detested coffee and had no regard for those that indulged in it. Bo would go out of his way to be sure to bring his one very hot, steaming cup of "Joe" each time he was ordered to appear.

Malory started with, "You know about this LaRoche thing, right?" Bo nodded in the affirmative. "Well you are on this case until it gets solved or people get tired of it. No ifs, ands, or buts. This one has got to be solved or forgotten real fast; I would prefer solved. The state is on my ass, and I'm gonna be on yours."

Bo started to ask a question, but the sheriff brushed it off with a wave of his hand. "You'll get what I think you need and no more, so don't go asking for any backup, fancy forensic tests, or anything else. I have other things to worry about besides those highfalutin beach people. So get out there and get me some answers quick. Any questions? I didn't think so."

Bo slowly rose from his seat. Malory watched the cup, not him, as if ready to pounce if he spilled one drop.

At the door, he turned and said, "Thanks, Sheriff," as he faked spilling the contents of the closely watched paper cup.

The sheriff gasped and clenched his teeth. "Get outta here!" he grumbled.

Outside the office Mary asked how it went. "Oh great!" he said. "I think he's warming up to me."

Mary gave a wry smile and chuckled. "He warms to no one. Now, what do you need? We have the blood type and some sample hair from Mr. LaRoche's home. The test won't be back on the arm for another four days, as if you needed it. And there are some people calling with tips, the usual ones: the gal on Oyster Factory that reports the aliens and always knows who did it, and Alvin Whetstone, the guy they arrest every week for drunk and disorderly, said he saw the whole thing, even though he's been in jail drying out for the last four days. But there is one that might have something. Suzy Fontana called and seemed a little anxious about some things she recently saw involving LaRoche."

Bo said, "Thanks, Mary, you're a doll," without looking up. He was staring at the slow drip from the bottom of his coffee cup.

Chapter 8

Investigation Begins

It was late morning when Bo arrived back on Edisto. Suzy Fontana was a single mom with three of the most beautiful girls you had ever seen. There was, however, a slight gap in ages—sixteen, six, and three—and they were all beautiful and smart. Tina, the youngest, had Edisto wrapped around her little finger. Everyone catered to her. Katie was the nature girl, who ran straight to the beach or woods and caught anything that moved. She had the unique ability to catch minnows and sometimes bigger fish in the surf with her bare hands. Kristine was the oldest. Smart and cute, she used her talents to land the editor position at the Walterboro High School newspaper. She would be a woman to reckon with some day.

Suzy worked at the Waterfront Restaurant and pulled both lunch and dinner shifts. Cecil LaRoche was one of her best customers. He came in about twice a week and always asked about her kids, her father,

Bobby Fontana, who owned Edisto Seafood, and her two brothers, Ashley and Barry, who helped their Dad. It was one of the old businesses on Edisto, and he always liked to hear what was going on with the business and the family. You could say he was smitten with her and not be far off.

But today she was off her usual self when the detective knocked on the door of her small home. She asked him in, and Kristine welcomed him with the obligatory heavy glass filled with ice and very sweet tea. The other girls came in smiled and said hello. He asked about school and grades, and then the older sister herded them into another room.

"So how have you been?" asked the detective.

"Just fine." She was never one to complain.

"So Mary said you called and might have some information about Cecile LaRoche," he said.

Suzy responded with, "Well, it might be nothing, but I did see Cecile at the Old Post Office a few Saturday nights ago. He was with some of his Edisto friends, you know, Cookie McKee, your brother, Pete Alexander, Sonny Cartwright, and another fellow I didn't know."

"So what made you think something was wrong?" he asked inquiringly.

"Nothing, until I thought about it. My date and I were walking behind them as we left the restaurant," she said. "Pete and Cookie chatted with Cecil and the other man a bit as they all stood outside. As we walked past, Cecil spoke and introduced everyone. He asked about the family, then we excused ourselves and walked on. I saw Pete and Cookie drive off in one car. That's when the other man I didn't know started to get loud and nasty with Cecil. We had arrived late, so we were parked on the far side next to the gift shop, out of their sight. My friend opened the car door for me, and as he closed it, I thought they were maybe gonna fight or something. The other guy was talking real mean to Cecil."

"I rolled down the window a bit and heard the other man say something like, 'This deal better go through, or it will be the last deal you ever make. You're into me up to your one good eyeball already, and I'm running out of time! I've played your game, and you are going to tell me where it is, now.'

"At first I didn't think too much about it, until we pulled out to drive down to the beach. That's when I saw what looked like a gun in the other man's hand, pointed at Cecil. A really big gun! I didn't say anything to my friend, but when I heard about Cecil's arm washing up, I decided I'd better call the sheriff's office."

"Well, you did the right thing," Bo told her.

"Well, the sheriff's department has always helped me when I needed it, so it's the least I can do," Suzy responded.

"Now you're sure of the others you saw that night?" asked the detective. She assured him that she knew all but the one man; however, she couldn't remember the stranger's name or much of a description of him.

He continued on with the questioning, and as he started to leave, she hesitated and he turned to look at her. She ducked her eyes and looked away, then crossed the room and opened a cabinet. She brought out a small cardboard box and held it close to her. She walked up to him, looked up, and handed him the box.

"What's this?"

"I don't know," she said with a bit of apprehension. "Cecil gave it to me. He said it was a gift. I didn't open it cause I was worried it might be something he shouldn't be giving me. He's married, and I don't want any trouble or people talking about me. I have enough of that already.

I decided to give it back to him and explain that we could only be friends. But I never saw him again," she explained with a pained look on her face.

"Well, maybe you should open it. It might help us find Cecil," he said.

"No, you open it. I don't want anything to do with it or Cecil or him disappearing or Shelby..." She began to rub her arms and pace the room. "You do what you want with it. Just leave me out of it. I don't need any more problems."

"We'll open it together." He pulled out his pocket knife and cut the tape on one end of the box. He tilted it over and caught a small metal object wrapped in brown paper.

She looked around without turning.

Bo slowly unwrapped it, held it in his hand, and turned it around several times. Then he tilted it in the light to read some stamped numbers along the edge. He shrugged his shoulders and looked confused. He hefted it to feel the weight, and then said to Suzy "Well, Cecil was kinda weird, but I don't think this was meant as a romantic gift."

She stepped over and took it from the big detective. "Now don't I feel pretty stupid? I thought Cecil was trying to come on to me. What a jerk. He had me worried for nothing. Well, what is it?"

"A joke, I think. If I know those clowns he was having dinner with, it has something to do with them picking on each other. Probably a part off of that boat they all own together; the one that never runs."

"If I ever see him again, I'm gonna take his glass eye for making me worry so much." She stopped and looked back. "You think he's alright? I mean, you think he's alive, right?"

He shrugged. "I don't know, Suzy, but we'll find him I'm sure. Don't worry. I won't tell anyone about your gift."

She laughed the laugh of someone who has been relieved of a great burden. "Thanks! Here, you keep it, and you can give it back to him," she said.

They laughed and talked some more as he walked out onto the porch.

He thanked her and she thanked him, and he left to go find those she saw at the restaurant that night.

Chapter 9

Interviews

Pete Alexander was in his office, a real estate office that closed down the previous year when the market went south, but he refused to move. Pete was a town councilman, a volunteer fireman, a real estate agent, and a pretty good liar. But everyone loved Pete, except for the other council members and the mayor. You could tell if it was Pete walking down the road from a mile away. He had the worst set of bowed legs in the state. One person was heard saying to him, "You couldn't catch a pig in a ditch with them legs."

The detective opened the door and leaned in. He started with the usual pleasantries: "You know, I can arrest you for trespassing." He stepped inside but didn't close the door.

Pete replied, "But you won't. Glad to see you too, Bo. So what can I do for you? Looking for a little bit of Cecil?"

"Well, yes and no" he replied. "I'm trying to find out what he was doing before he disappeared and who he's been hangin' around with. Had you seen him lately?"

"Well, me, Cookie, and Sonny had dinner with him and some guy at the Old Post Office Restaurant recently. One of the best steaks I have ever had, by the way. So that would have been, what? A few days before all this happened."

"Was it just you three?"

"No, I said some guy was with him."

"Well, who was he?"

"I don't remember," Pete replied, defensively with his voice rising. "Just another one of Cecil's friends that he always has. I think he said he was from Camden or Sumter. Another developer gonna build out on Point of Pines Road. I didn't think much of him, so I blew him off."

"You didn't get his name?

"No, no, I'm sure he told me, but I forgot. Anyway, no one will ever be able to develop that land. The Fire Ant Preservation Group will stop any affordable housing being built on Edisto Island anyway. So I wasn't interested in buyin' what he was sellin'. But it was some real common name, actually too common, like John Smith, I think. Sonny or Cookie might remember. Ask them."

"I will," he said. They changed the subject and talked on a bit, and then the detective drove to Sonny Cartwright's office less than a half of a mile away. It, too, was a piece of work. In the back of Bill Haskell's insurance office were two offices kind of "thrown up." The walls didn't reach the ceiling, but they had locks on the doors and a desk and two chairs in each one. It made for a noisy place sometimes when everyone was on the phone. One belonged to Sonny and the other belonged to Bo McKee's brother, Cookie McKee. As Bo walked past

Cookie's office, he waved to him since he was on the phone, tapped on Sonny's door, and let himself in. In one of the two chairs, the most uncomfortable-looking one, sat Duncan Callaway, the local manager of the Entrepreneur Bank of Edisto. Duncan hadn't been working as a banker around Edisto Beach long, but he had a vacation house close to the beach and got tapped for the branch when an opening came up. He and Sonny were longtime friends and had been in each other's weddings.

The Entrepreneur Bank of Edisto, like so many things on Edisto, had its own little secrets and ways of doing business—like the time the robbers broke into the vault on a Sunday before church. They drove down to Steamboat Landing and pushed their getaway car down the boat ramp to sink it. They had a boat tied up to the floating dock and waiting for them because they knew the first thing the cops would do would be to open the old swing bridge at the Intracoastal Waterway and stop all of the traffic. But they couldn't outrun the radios; game wardens had them from an airplane before the boat turned out into the North Edisto. The robbers had been helped by the local electrician, a teller's husband, working on the lights in the safe.

Also, some questionable loans had been made by Bernie Horton, the previous manager; while not illegal, they were suspicious at best. From continuing to finance one businessman that was up to his eyeballs in tax evasion, to the old man that was charged 26 percent on a ninety day note to buy an old, worn-out, overpriced pickup truck from the banker's nephew. Some loans were just not loans but favors to friends and relatives. But the bank's board of directors got wind of it, and Bernie resigned right quick.

Duncan came in and cleaned house. He, too, had become one of Edisto's best. If you could prove you could repay your loan, you got it.

If you got in trouble with your loan, all you had to do was come see him, and he would do all he could to help.

He asked Bo about the investigation and then left.

Sonny Cartwright was another Edisto character. He built houses, and he did a fine job of it. He was meticulous in his work and demanded perfection. He drove everyone crazy—the home owner, the contractors, the building inspectors, even his lovely wife, Rose. People would always say, "She has the patience of Job," and she would have to. She had been married for forty-two years to "Mr. Persnickety."

Like Pete Alexander, Sonny didn't remember much about the fellow Cecil brought to dinner that night. He said the same things about the development of the Point of Pines track and that it would never happen. But he did add one thing: the guy had on a USC hat and ring, but the colors were all wrong. It turned out he was a graduate from The University of Southern California. He and several of his alma mater friends had come to Edisto for a reunion of sorts and were looking for investment opportunities.

Then he suddenly remembered. His name was Robert Smith, and he lived in Dalzell between Camden and Sumter (all in South Carolina). Sonny recalled his disposition was a little aggressive and edgy, not the kind of person Cecil hung around with often. But it was real estate, and you meet all kinds of people in that business. He said he had also seen this same guy coming out of Al Cabella's real estate office earlier that day but didn't know of any deals that might be going on. He just thought he was probably looking for investors and supporters for his development project. Bo thanked Sonny and stepped across the way to see his brother, Cookie.

Cookie McKee was always a delightful man. He worked hard and played even harder. He knew everywhere to hunt and fish and always brought home food for the family. The family consisted of himself, his wife, Sarah Anne, and two beautiful daughters, Mary Evelyn and Maggy. Both girls excelled in college and in breaking hearts. But today Cookie was not his usual self—all smiles and full of cheer (it was sickening at times).

"What's the problem, bro?" Bo had heard he was distraught over a deal that fell through.

"The buyer went for another property," said Cookie. "I was so sure I had this piece sold, that I had obligated the funds. Now I have to go back and tell this other guy I don't have the money. It's generally not that big of a deal, but with the recession and real estate not selling very well on Edisto, everyone needs any money they can get."

Bo asked, "So what cha gonna do?"

Cookie, with his wry smile, answered, "Call Duncan and see if he'll give me a deal.

"He was just talking to Sonny before I came in here, ya know."

"Yeah, I saw him leave, but the best way to make a deal with Duncan is over breakfast at the Sea Cow. The grits and sausage gravy mellow him out." Bo asked a few more questions, then asked about his wife and kids. Their dad passed away years before, and they were good sons. They kept an eye out and helped their mom regularly.

Bo said goodbye and left, promising to come for Sunday dinner.

Chapter 10

Not Much

Not much to go on, thought the detective. An arm, a mystery man, and just now a dark blue van rolling out of town that said: "U.S. Government—Scientific Testing—Iodine, Nickel, Kinetic Systems."

"US. GOVERNMENT STINKS?" He laughed to himself. Maybe that was some kind of sign. If it was, then he knew he had to find the mystery man to get anywhere with this case.

He went straight to the source of all information on Edisto, Jack Hosley. But unbeknownst to Bo, Jack had been in the hospital for the past four weeks and had nothing of importance pertaining to the case. So he listened patiently to Jack complain first and then reminisce about the land in Iceland that he won in a poker game in the 70s. Then, when he finished the war stories, become outraged at Bo because he hadn't solved the case in twenty-four hours. So why was he sitting in his living room when there was a murderer on the loose?

"Go do your job!" yelled Hosley.

Bo thanked Jack's wife, Dee, and left. Jack watched as he backed out onto Jungle Road and almost ran over a tourist driving a golf cart. Then he turned to Dee and said, "I still got it! I can get under their skin, just like in the old days."

To which she replied, "Not just theirs, dear. Not just theirs."

Chapter 11

Realtors

So with no more than he had when he started, other than a headache, he went looking for Al Cabella. The real estate office was open, but Al was nowhere to be found.

Miss Caroline Ottman explained that Al always goes to Charleston on Tuesdays for an appointment. She would not explain further, but one of the other realtors made a snide remark as he walked by: "But Al's always in a better mood when he returns."

Al Cabella started his real estate career in the little blue building at highway 174 and Steamboat Landing Road, now occupied by Flower's Seafood. He, Cecil LaRoche, and Jim Campbell shared the little building and a single phone. There were their regular customers, who came by each day and would sit, read the one copy of the Charleston paper, and never buy a single piece of real estate. They stayed longer on Mondays to read the Sunday paper as well. All of them had their self-appointed time, and if someone read a little slower than the others, they would divide what was already read and keep the cycle going. Al built a good business and was doing well until the bottom fell out. Like all of the realtors, now he was just trying to hold on to what he had.

Bo nodded at the tall man behind the other desk. This day, Campbell was busy working hard to help some of the older retirees who had gotten caught when the taxes and insurance went through the roof to sell their dream homes and relocate to a cheaper area inland. His signature Day-Timer was filled with the pink phone message notes that Sue Morton, his secretary, gave him every time he walked through the door. He was the one you went to to sell your house. Mary Bobitt was the one you went to to buy a house, and that was his next stop.

It was a nice day, and the door was open wide at Bobitt Home Sales. Felesse NaVidia was standing at the front desk when he came up the steps. He remembered seeing her at the Governor's Cup Fishing Tournament with her new beau. They seemed like a very happy twenty-something-year-old couple. He asked if Mary was in, and she said, "No, she's out showing houses to prospective buyers just like she always does." But she offered, "Jerome is in, but he's on the phone."

He replied, "That's who I wanted to see, anyway." Jerome Kromer was Mary's husband and business partner. Just then the light on her phone went off.

She said, "You better get upstairs to his office quick if you want to catch him before he gets on it again."

Bo bounded up the stairs and stuck his nose around the corner. Jerome looked a little perturbed but motioned him in.

"Bo, what are you up to? Did you find anymore of Cecil?"

Bo gave a breathless reply: "No, and those stairs will kill ya! I'm trying to find out about this Robert Smith guy and the development on Point of Pines."

"You mean the one that will never fly?"

"Why do you say that?"

"The freakin' Fire Ants. They stop everything to do with building around here. I understand it was supposed to be something like affordable track homes for people who work on Edisto Beach," Jerome said with disdain. "How are the people that work here supposed to live here? It's that damn David Canton. He's got his piece of paradise, so now it's 'blow up the bridge' and don't let anybody else come to Edisto!"

"What about Smith?" queried Bo.

"I don't know anything about him, and none of my contacts around the state have heard of him either. I already asked about him for you. A little puzzling for a guy trying get $2.6 million in investment for affordable housing."

"Did he go to the bank?"

"Don't know, but he better have his ducks in a row before he goes to Duncan. The Entrepreneur Bank of Edisto is strictly by the book these days, and collateral is the name of the game."

"So what about the new bank, First Federal?"

"A Walterboro bank that was trying to cash in on the real estate boom on the beach before real estate went bust. Nothing to do with the bank, but the prices of houses have dropped and the taxes and insurance have gone up, so nobody's buying anything right now. Good people, though. I've sent a few over to see them, but they, too, are by the book."

"So this guy needed to find friends with cash?"

"What cash? No one has cash. All of the investment cash on Edisto went down with the stock market."

"Did Cecil have any cash to invest?"

"I wouldn't think so. He was doing alright before the bottom fell out. But remember—when Cecil LaRoche came back to Edisto years ago, he was a man with only a beat-up truck, a mangy old dog, and $20,000 in cattle debt."

"What's cattle debt?"

"Debt you owe someone for the cattle you probably paid too much for and you sold for less than what you paid originally. Most of the time you pay a percentage of the agreed price for the young livestock, then you fatten them up. Depending on how much you sell them for, you give a portion of the profit to the original owner, the agreed difference, and pocket the rest. Or you go back with your tail between your legs and ask for an extension or some other way to pay off the debt. In most cases it ends up costing you and arm and a leg."

Jerome thought about it for a minute and a smile gradually broke out as he said, "Well, Cecil has paid for some of it I guess!" Then he broke into an outrageous laugh. "Sorry, sorry I couldn't help myself," he said as he wiped away the tears.

Just then Felesse poked her head up from the stairs and, looking through the banister, called to Bo and said, "Mr. Bo, you better come downstairs. Someone wants to see you real bad."

He stood up, looked at Jerome as he was still trying to regain his composure, shook his head, and went down stairs.

"Who wants to see me, Felesse?" he asked.

"He's outside in the black truck."

Bo looked out the window, saw who it was, and looked quickly for an escape route. There was none! He was trapped. Even if he were able to sneak away, leave his car, and walk the three miles home, he would still be seen exiting the back of the building. Nothing he could do but face the inevitable. He slowly walked down the steps, watching the big black Suburban with the low rumbling of a worn-out muffler. He knew the threat it posed, and dread was locked on his face. Just as he got to the driver's side, the black-tinted window came down with a thud.

"I gotta fix that someday," said the large white-haired man with the bulbous nose.

It was Neuron Fornsby. Big and tall, he was always sporting a smile that made you wonder if it was real or not. His mother was a big fan of *Bill Nye the Science Guy* and named him Neuron after some fancy word she had heard on his TV show. Neuron, however, was not into science but was heavily into the nefarious ways of the human psyche. In other words, he was the biggest conspiracy freak you'd ever met. Everything was a conspiracy! The Piggly Wiggly was conspiring to double the price of bananas even though there was a glut of them in the world market. He listened to every radio talk show and could recite verse from all of them. "The president was a socialist and had the tattoos between his toes to prove it." The people at town hall would suddenly disappear when they saw him coming. There was always a traffic jam at the back door as everyone tried to escape.

"So have you heard about the rest of Cecil's body? It turned up at Savannah!" he said, beaming. "It's true! Popped up right there at River Street in front of that big Hilton Hotel there," he said with pride and conviction.

"And who told you this?" asked Bo, looking a little more than perturbed.

"Well, I can't tell you." he said with a pause. "Just like a reporter. Yeah! Just like Percy Mason at the Standard Press. I have to protect my sources." He looked as if Bo was trying to cheat off his paper in a spelling test in third grade.

"Well, it's no good to me if I can't verify it."

"You got a radio. Call it in. Ask them cops down there. Oh! Or maybe they are in on it too! Damn, I didn't think of that. Gotta go!" He grabbed what was still showing of the window and pulled it up to close it. He sped away holding the window with his right hand and trying to drive with his left.

Chapter 12

Dockside

Bo had spent the day calling everywhere and trying to get a search warrant for Cecil's office to look for the stranger's fingerprints to check them against the national registry. He was hoping that this mystery man might already have a record and that his prints could identify him quickly. After that he went to the Edisto Marina and Pressley's Grill and looked at tide charts and currents, trying to get some of the fishermen to help him determine where the arm may have come from. But there were too many variables to be sure of that.

It was getting to be late afternoon. He left and drove out of the parking lot by the golf course and to the Dockside Lounge. The old Dockside regulars were there, and everyone acknowledged him as he came in. Almost all of them had a history with him, as he had arrested most them at least once. He sat on the left side of the bar thinking, *What a dump.* It wasn't dirty, just stale and old, and the ceiling was only about six and a half feet high. The walls were covered with bumper stickers and decals from years of people just putting up random stuff. The pinball machine still had the Don't Work sign on it. It was getting pretty ragged after three years of fending off would-be gamers.

Mary Evelyn, his niece, came up and asked, "What ya' drinking, Uncle Bo? I guess you're off of those slow gin fizz things after last Christmas, eh?" Cookie made a big pitcher of them, and he had over indulged. But he figured he had a right to. The sheriff was ready to string him up for his getting a "confession" from "Dancing Dave" Morrison.

It seems that he picked up Dave Morrison after he fell off the bicycle he was riding home from some drinking establishment. While he had him in the car, he got "Dancing Dave" to confess to stealing Larry Martin's motorized post-hole digger. There were only two on the island, and someone saw Dave trying to crank one over by the elementary school. So a quick stop on top of the McKinley Washington Jr. Bridge (over seventy feet down to the water) got old Dave a talking. Hanging by the back of his belt over the long drop to the muddy water below made him remember a lot of things—like where all of the stuff he had stolen was stashed. Of course, Morrison had no witnesses to the abusive interrogation, so he couldn't press charges against the officer, but everyone knew it could be true.

Little Miss Mev (Mary Evelyn) brought Bo a Pabst Blue Ribbon and a frosted cold glass. It was 98 degrees outside, so the glass was more for show because as hot as it was, it didn't do much good. But she was smart, and it made the patrons feel better and in turn tip better.

"So how's the investigation going?" she asked.

"Slow but steady. Trying to find out about a guy named Robert Smith. He came from around Camden or Sumter and was talking to Cecil about developing the land at the end of Point of Pines."

"Tall guy, kinda lanky set?"

"Well, that's more than I've been able to get so far."

"Ask your other niece; she said there was some creepy guy that rented a boat from her over at Edisto Watersports just before it all happened," Mev offered.

"What made him creepy?" he asked.

"Not sure, but she's still over there washing down the boats, cause I heard some guys whistling."

"Thanks, Mev," he said, and he got up to leave. She looked at him as if he might be trying to skip out on his tab. He turned and tossed a twenty-dollar bill on the counter. "Happy birthday"

She smiled. "Thanks, it was four months ago," she said and bounced off to the register.

Maggy was talking to Captain Jamie Springer, one of the younger charter captains, and washing down the last kayak as he walked up.

"Hey, Uncle Bo!" she said, beaming as she tried to squirt him with the hose.

"Watch it, kid. A taser and water don't mix," he laughed.

"Hey, Springer, you looking after my niece or looking at her?

"A little of both, Mr. McKee. You doin alright?"

"Yeah, a little busy these days," said the detective.

"I guess so with that LaRoche thing and all. Hey, Maggy, I'll see you later at Bingo, OK? You want me to pick you up?"

"No, I'll get a ride with Margaret, and we'll meet you there."

Maggy's rejection of the offered ride showed on Springer's face, but he did his best to hide it as he walked back to Edisto Seafood.

Chapter 13

Springer

They always flocked to her at the dockside bar, the vultures. Maggy was good at fending most of them off, but one night this guy just wouldn't give up. His original small talk had become more suggestive and aggressive. Tall, with a "football build" and a little tipsy, he wouldn't be a problem for Jamie Springer. With the skills he learned from the local sensei master Marion Whaley (the younger), Springer could handle anything that came to Edisto.

Springer was a quiet type; no one ever noticed him, but strangely, he always seemed to be there when anyone needed help or just to talk. He had a great disarming smile and was wiry but strong—a good friend to have in good times and bad.

He handled this one as he had the others. When Maggy turned to speak to one of her friends, Captain J. Springer bumped the guy hard with his left shoulder. As his target turned, a quick flick of his left fingers caught the gonads, and the target lurched forward. Springer's right hand, with the thumb as a dagger, hit the trifecta region of the neck. The combination of the impact on the jugular vein, nerve, and muscle caused the man to collapse like a wet rag. Springer motioned to the bartender, who knew what was going on, and he quickly found the guy's friends and told them to take their drunken friend out before he called the cops to haul all of them away.

Maggy simply stepped back as they gathered their stunned friend and carried him outside. One was saying something about he could never handle hard liquor as the other apologized for his friend.

She turned to Springer, who was looking at his beer, and said, "Those Aiken boys can't hold a drink." Springer looked at her and smiled. He gave a quick nod in agreement and then walked out on the covered deck.

Chapter 14

Maggy Lost It

"I think he likes you," said her uncle.

"Springer? Springer? I've beat his ass so many times growing up that he's just scared of me. That's why he acts all weird sometimes," she laughed.

"Your sister said there was a creepy guy that rented a boat from you," he said as they walked inside.

"Which one? They all seem to be all creepy this year. Oh yeah, it was a week or so ago, but he was different creepy, nothing I could really put my finger on, but he just acted funny. Looked at me all weird and stuff," she said with a shudder.

"Well, if you wore more clothes, everyone would stop looking at you so weird," he said in a paternal voice. She always wore a small bikini top and jean shorts that she cut way up high. But she was young, and she pulled it off incredibly well.

"Oh, you and my dad are always complaining about how I dress. Most men don't say anything."

"Guess not. They're tongue tied after seeing you hanging out of that outfit," he said as she looked around for the receipt book.

"I save money on clothes," she said as she reached over the counter to get the book, showing even more.

He looked away. "So what did you get on him with the rental?"

"The usual information from his license: name, address, driver's license number. But he paid cash for the rental and used cash for the deposit," she said as she thumbed through the book. "That's unusual, especially when it's for a business."

"What do you mean?" asked the detective.

"He mentioned a business name. I forgot what it was. But, Bo, wouldn't you use a credit card to keep track of your receipts so you could get reimbursed or write it off?" She started to look puzzled.

"What's wrong?"

"My copy is gone. The yellow one I keep for Lauren is not in the book," she explained as she looked around the counter. "If Donald has been in this book I'm gonna kill him. That's if Lauren doesn't kill me first."

Donald and Lauren Long bought Edisto Watersports four years ago. It was a nice little business that rented kayaks, small inflatable boats and on occasion the 18 foot mako center console.

"Well while you're looking to save your butt, where did the guy go?"

Getting more frantic in her search she said,"Otter Island. He had two big waterproof cases. Like Pelican cases, you know the real expensive ones. I asked him if I could help him load them in the boat and he said 'No' and I asked him if he needed a guide. And again he said 'No' and held up a GPS. Springer was over at the Fontana dock and he knows those islands better than anyone or any GPS. But he insisted on doing everything himself. So I let him."

"Did he say what he was doing out there?" he queried.

She hollered from the back office, "Said he was looking for good water for the town. It's not here," she said flatly. "Somebody took it! And they are going to pay with their ass for that! Somebody is trying to make me look bad, and that ain't gonna fly." She stomped around the room looking in places it would never be.

"What makes you think someone took it?" he asked.

"Because it has no value to anyone but me and Lauren. All that missing piece of paper can do is make my life miserable." She started to get louder. "And when I find who did it, their ass is grass, and I'm gonna be the lawnmower."

The detective let her rant, then offered, "It just might be more valuable missing than you think. Was Mr. Smith in here alone for any length of time?" he asked with a slight smile.

"No. Well, yeah, when he came back. I went to fill up the gas tanks on the boat after he came back. I had to charge him for the gas he used. He was in here on his cell phone but only for a minute. He came outside complaining about the cell service and walked over to the sign where the service is better. You think he took it?" she asked.

"Don't know. See you later. Get some clothes," he called back as he walked quickly to his car that was making a weird buzzing sound announcing he had a radio message coming in. Just as he started the gray unmarked car, his radio came to life. The dispatcher, Sue Walker, who had been his high school math teacher, said the search warrant had been issued and signed, and the crime scene unit would be at Cecil's office 9:00 a.m. the next day. Bo started to pull out, and a golf cart almost hit him.

Chapter 15

Drive by Boat

At Edisto Seafood, the Fontana brothers were at it again. Ashley Fontana was trying to sleep off a hangover in an old plastic lounge chair at the end of the dock behind the shrimp boats. He was hoping his father, Bobby Fontana, was too busy to look for him. Barry Fontana had been working on the Red Eye sport fisher boat for days. He had missed a number of charters and was anxious to get the boat running again so as not to miss the entire tourist season. As he backed the big boat in, Hubby Combine came up with a beer in one hand and caught the line thrown to him with the free one to secure the boat to the dock. He looked at Barry, then at Ashley sleeping on the chaise lounge. The chair was right on top of the cleat that Hubby needed to tie the line to. So there was nothing to do but tie the boat up to the end of the sleeping man's chair. He stepped on board to lend a hand. About that same time, Bobby Fontana came around the shrimp boat, Sarah Jane, and hollered loudly at both boys.

"What the hell are ya'll doing? There's work to be done around here, and you need to get your lazy asses to doing it. This ain't Disney World!"

The yelling startled Barry, who turned around and stepped right into Hubby and his beer. Off-balance Barry fell back, caught onto the T top, and swung himself around the console. Hubby wasn't so lucky. He fell across and into the controls of the idling boat. The engines seemed to stall, which would have been good for Ashley, but when they caught and sprang to life, the boat lifted like a scared marsh hen and took off straight up Big Bay Creek with Ashley in tow, sitting on the lounge chair.

Ashley was white as a new-made sail and holding on for dear life. The legs of the chair had sheared off when the boat pulled him off the dock. Remarkably, the chair was planing like a surfboard and doing pretty good. Barry swung back around the hardtop and bumped Hubby off the controls. He started a long sweeping turn just before Yacht Basin. A little more throttle, and the chair banked on the wake and maintained the plane through the turn. Ashley, finally coming to his senses, began to lean and move the improvised wakeboard beyond the wake and closer to the docks. As the Red Eye passed the Sarah Jane, he grabbed a net hanging from the boom and swung aboard. Will Smoakes, captain of the Sarah Jane, was not amused. Neither was Bobby Fontana and he started letting them know it as soon as he was sure everyone was OK.

"What kind of foolish stunt was that? You could have killed your brother."

Every time one of them tried to say something in their defense he would start again. He stayed on them for quite a while until the black Contender eased by. Everyone stopped and looked. It was like a picture from a glossy magazine. A beautiful boat captained by a beautiful woman in a small black bikini, her long black hair flying in the breeze. The rednecks on the screened porch at the Dockside Lounge looked (and sounded) like the Monkey's on Morgan Island.

Morgan Island was also known as Monkey Island. Retired laboratory monkeys that had survived science experiments were allowed to live out their lives on the island undisturbed.

But they had more manners than these guys. The beautiful lady in her beautiful boat just waved and continued on her way. When she made the turn at Yacht Basin and out of the no wake zone, she opened up the big motors and broke a lot of hearts.

The boat handled nicely through the sharp turns and right up and into the abandoned boat house on Fishing Creek. She stepped off the deck and hit the switch to close the electric door and hide the boat. The Contender was raised from the water on a powerful lift and she hosed it off quickly. The boathouse had been refitted by a construction crew from Beaufort, and no one knew she bought it and refurbished the inside. On the outside it still looked like an old relic of days gone by. Inside there were all the comforts of home, a little crowded but serviceable. She took a long, hot shower and tried to calm herself and forget the past.

Chapter 16

The Old Camper—Will Goes Down

Dan Shorter noticed the old Datsun pickup camper was parked by the Pavilion again that morning. He and his friend Dom (Dominic) Marsala had spoken many times about the mystery "old camper man" that came to Edisto about once or twice a year. They made up stories over their morning coffee for years about the rough-looking character. At times they would suggest that he was an author or a secret millionaire. They had no clue, but they enjoyed the game. However, they were both very wrong. The mystery "camper man" had been scouting around Edisto Beach for the better part of four years. This morning his walk was a little faster as he approached the old Datsun pickup with the camper on the back. He took a quick look around, then opened the door and quickly entered. Inside the small space was the constant hum of electronics. Satellite radios and short-wave transmitters with their antennas hidden under the cargo container on top kept the small space hot. The little twelve-volt air conditioner struggled to keep up. Computers with cell connections displayed images and data from all over the beach. The small cameras were looking for someone or something. The young man who had made himself up to look much older than his actual thirty-two years studied the monitors again. But he needed more batteries and something to eat. He decided to head across the street to the gas station and McConkey's Jungle Shack for the fried pork ribs and beer. He closed the camper's door as he slid on his rainbow sandals, but the latch didn't click completely, and he had other things on his mind anyway as he crossed Palmetto Boulevard.

Sweet William was strolling along the beach again looking for shells, sharks' teeth, and available men. He passed the old camper man earlier in the day and offered a quick hello. He was getting lonely and thought maybe even if the old guy didn't want to fool around, he might be up for some conversation. He mustered his courage and tapped lightly on the door of the old camper. No one answered. He turned to walk away dejected, but then he heard the creaking of the door as it slowly swung open. Smiling, he turned to face the stranger from the camper...who wasn't there.

The whirling sounds of electronics fascinated the amateur computer geek, and curiosity got the best of him. He looked around and saw there was no one looking in his direction, so he edged a little closer, just to look inside. Suddenly, there was a sharp pain behind his right ear and the floor came up to meet him.

Chapter 17

Cecil's Office and the Pig

The next morning when Bo arrived, the team was finishing up with checking for fingerprints on doors and drawers and looking at the computer drives. Cecil wasn't into anything weird on his computer, but he really liked comics. He had all kinds of shortcuts and favorites that lead to comic strips. There where tons of pictures on the walls, a belt buckle from his rodeo days, and a mallard hen mounted. Most people mounted the drake as it was much more colorful. *Different*, thought the detective. There were pictures on top of each other, and you had to move one to see another. As he was poking thought the stuff, Dan Shorter came to the door, tapped lightly, and asked if he could be of any help.

Dan Shorter was the executive director of the Edisto Beach Chamber of Commerce, and his office was in the same small building. He was also anything else you needed him to be regarding the Chamber of Commerce. He was the only employee. Tall, slim, and gray, he looked distinguished for an Edistonian. He was always properly starched and dressed, and today he was smiling just like the day before and the day before that. Bo asked him when he last saw Cecil.

"Friday before last, I think. Yes it was. I have been out of town on a business trip to Orlando and to see my daughter who lives there too," he said in his polite way.

"You drive that old Jeep Cherokee all that way?" he asked.

"Why, yes. Betsy can make any trip to anywhere."

"How many miles you got on that thing?"

"About 897,000 I think. I don't look. I'm too scared it might make a difference in where I would feel comfortable to drive the thing. I'm having some confidence problems with her lately. She blew the radiator cap gasket, and I had to make a new one out of cardboard. It's holding so far," he said showing his crossed fingers.

"Any ideas about our friend Cecil?"

"No, he was always working on one more big deal. He would never say what they were, just that this was the big one, and it would put him over the top. He could retire and hunt and fish the rest of his life."

"Did you see or meet a Mr. Robert Smith that Cecil was dealing with?"

"No, as I said I've been gone for over a week," Shorter explained.

"Well, that's who I'm looking for. If you hear of him, let me know, will ya?"

"Sure, I'll keep an eye out for him," he said, ducking his head and looking rather embarrassed.

"What?" asked the lawman with a confused look.

Shorter explained, "Eye out. Cecil's left eye, ya know? Glass eye?"

Bo just shook his head, and Shorter left with a muffled laugh.

The phone rang on the cluttered desk. Everyone stopped and looked at the detective, then at each other. Bo reached across the chair and picked it up. He listened carefully and made a surprised look as he listened. He didn't say a thing but slowly turned to each one of the crime scene investigators, looking astonished as he did. Everyone stood perfectly still and didn't dare make a sound. He turned the phone so the mouth piece was high in the air, still listening to the receiver.

"Bucks Pizza is out of feta cheese. Ya'll want extra parmesan?" he asked loudly. "Greek wedding party in town got the good stuff."

Everyone in the room got a perturbed look on their face, shook their heads, and went back to work. The supervisor said the parmesan would do. He hung up the phone. And it rang again as soon as he let it go. He looked at the phone again with a strange look on his face. No one was falling for it this time. It was the coroner's office saying they had some news about the arm and that he should come to Walterboro to meet with the coroner and the sheriff right away.

So off to Walterboro he went. He drove the forty-five minutes, thinking about anything but Cecil LaRoche. George Jones was on his iPod, and he didn't see the silver Land Rover parked at a peculiar angle at Martin's Market. As he passed Eddingsville Beach Road, it pulled out and followed him at a distance until he was going over the McKinley Bridge that spanned the North Edisto. It slowed down after he went over the top and pulled over to the side. After he passed the osprey's nest on the last utility pole, it did a very illegal U-turn and headed back toward Edisto Beach.

At the coroner's office there were pictures of what was left of Cecil's arm. Most were close-ups of the part that should have been connected to his upper arm.

Dr. Joe Bowers, local MD and chairman of Colleton County Council, said, "As you can see, the detachment was at the elbow." Bo had to hide his smile. "The separation was not performed by a sharp object." The doctor pointed to several photos.

"Well, what was it if it wasn't a knife?" asked the sheriff, who was quickly tiring of the theatrics.

"I'm not sure, but if you look closely…"

It was Bo's turn to get pissed off. "Just tell us what you think happened. We've still got to try to find the rest of him. And could he have survived losing that part of his arm?"

"Well, the second question is the easiest. Yes, if there had been any way to stop the bleeding if he were alive when the separation occurred. However, from the clotting that I have been able to see, I would say he was in the water when it happened or right after he was relieved of this appendage."

"So someone or something tore his arm off in the water?" said Bo, exasperated by the doctor.

"Or right before. Tore it off, that is my conclusion. But I will need to conduct more tests."

"Nope, you're not running up a big bill with the medical university doing tests on my watch. Wrap it up and stuff it in the freezer over at the jail. Make sure you label it good so one of those nutty cooks doesn't try to fry it. Then write up what you said in simple terms, and send it to me." The sheriff was almost out of the door.

"Detective, a word!" The Sheriff shouted over the roar of a passing truck. "Where are you with this? No bullshit, just tell me what you got."

"Right now not much. Cecil was apparently involved with some guy named Robert Smith, who was working on developing a big tract of land that the old farts on the beach didn't want developed. This Smith rented a small boat, and he went over to Otter Island looking for good drinking water for the town. But the receipt from where he rented the boat, with all of his driver's license information, is missing."

"Misplaced or stolen?" asked the sheriff.

"Looking like he might have taken it when no one was looking."

"OK. Stay on it. And don't embarrass me."

Bo walked slowly back to his car. His personal cell phone chimed in with the Cops TV show theme. It was Jack Hosley.

"Where the hell are you? I need you here now!"

"What's the big emergency, Jack?"

"I've got two people who called in and can't help with bingo at the Lions Club. I need you here by 6:00 to call out the numbers for the bingo games."

"Well, it's 5:15, and I'm in Walterboro, so that just ain't gonna happen."

"Well, you better get here and get here quick. I can't do the whole thing myself. At the next board meeting I'm gonna tell them exactly that. All of them. You can bet your ass. This is ridiculous…" he said, and his voice trailed off.

"OK, OK, I'll get there as soon as I can," Bo yelled back into the fading signal. His gray unmarked Chevy Malibu pulled out of the parking lot, the driver still looking for golf carts.

On the way back to Edisto, Bo reflected on the irony of the events.

He had been a Colleton County deputy on Edisto for three years when he got the promotion to detective. It meant more money, of course, but it also meant he didn't have to work the late shift unless something came up. He liked having his time off at night. He was able to go to a nice dinner, hang out with friends, and even join the Lions

Club. The Edisto Island Lions Club was a unique little group. They recently allowed women to join, and about a quarter of the members resigned in protest. When he joined, one of the members came up to him and said it was nice to have young people join the club. He looked around, and sure enough, he was one of the younger people in the room. He also found out later that at fifty-six he really was the youngest member.

Suddenly, he ran into a traffic jam on Highway 174 just past Roxbury Mercantile Restaurant. The traffic that normally ran at sixty miles per hour began to slow and then came to a crawl. There was a line of cars, at least ten or twelve of them, all following Miss Janie McCollum in her little gray Toyota, doing forty miles per hour. Highway 174 has only a few places where it is safe to pass another car. There was no way he was going to get to the Lions Club on time. He thought about turning on the blue lights, but he knew Miss McCollum would never pull over, and if the sheriff found out, he would be in even more trouble. So he drove eleven cars behind her like everyone else and cursed the two-lane road.

When he got to Eddingsville Beach Road, it was already after 6:00. His phone had been going off, but he knew better than to answer it. As he made the turn, he hit the gas, and the tires slid a little on the shell sand road, and the car drifted sideways. He straightened out and punched it again. Only he and one other part-time neighbor ever used the road, so it was pretty much his private driveway. As he took the second curve at George & Pink's vegetable stand, he saw a huge wild pig standing in the middle of the road facing him. It was too late. He couldn't miss the pig, and the startled pig was not going to move.

The car's bumper hit the three-hundred-pound bovine just below the chest and flipped him head over heels over the hood of the car. His rear hooves came through the windshield. The glass collapsed from the impact, and the airbag deployed and blew back straight into the driver's seat instead of upward. The bag and the pig caught him in the chest. The impact broke the seat loose from the floor of the car and pushed him into the back seat. The car was still moving and slid hard into a two-hundred-year-old grand oak, bounced off, and spun twice.

Bo couldn't breathe. The pig's butt was right on top of him. He couldn't move to get out, and those mountain oysters in his face where smelling a might frightful. Luckily, the pig was dead. Had he started moving those hooves, the detective would have looked much different the rest of his life. There were sounds of people around him. And someone grabbed the pig and pulled it out of the car. Another started pulling the windshield out of the way. He was able to move enough to get his knife and cut the seat belt. There was plenty of room for him to get out now, but his left leg wouldn't move, then it started to hurt—and hurt bad. He could see blood all around him, but he wasn't sure if it was his or the pig's. When he looked up, there was Warren Kaczynski, the painter, staring down at him.

"Are you alright, Bo? You look a bit beat up from here. What hurts?"

"I'm not sure, but my left leg won't move," he said with a grimace.

"Pink's called 911, so EMS will be here in just a minute. Just wait and let them help you out. I can't see any cuts on you, but there is a lot of blood. It must be the pig's."

"I haven't seen any pigs around here. Where the hell did he come from?" He grimaced in serious pain.

"I don't know, but the Mexicans got him now. They done loaded him up on their old pickup and took off," Warren explained.

The EMS truck arrived and started working on him. Warren stepped back to get out of the way. That's when he noticed a pile of corn in the middle of the road. Not corn still on the cob but shelled corn in a pile about a foot across. It was a neat little pile, except where the hog had started eating. Pugzie, Warren's bulldog, started making noises on the side of the road. Warren went over to get him and put him back in the truck. But Pugzie was onto something. He was sniffing and scratching and carrying on. Warren stepped across the ditch and saw where someone had been putting a lot of feed out. There were only traces now, but it was evident that someone had been feeding the wildlife right next to the road behind the silver maples that grew in the ditch. Warren looked back at the road and then back at the ground he was standing on, and then he scratched his head thoughtfully.

Chapter 18

About Cecil and His tale

Warren drove to Whaley's Store and sidled up to his usual spot. He didn't say much and didn't have to. The whole crowd was talking about Bo McKee being flown by helicopter to St. Francis Hospital. It was always a big deal when they had to close the driving range for the air ambulance guys.

Once, a golfer refused to stop hitting golf balls as the Medivac helicopter approached. Deputy Bobby Hanson took out his police shotgun and blew up the next ball the guy hit, just like at the skeet range. The pale, irate golfer left quickly. Bobby was like that.

But Warren Kaczynski was thinking years before and miles away.

Dr. Randolph Kaczynski, Warren's father, was an emanate professor in the study of dyslexia and other learning disabilities. Warren had gone beyond medical science and into the field of modern history, particularly the great wars. He was intrigued by the motivations of evil men. His research and conclusions took him all the way to Oxford

University in England. Then suddenly, without explanation, he resigned and came back to Charleston, South Carolina.

His father retired from research and took a position as the headmaster at The Aiken Academy Middle School in Aiken, South Carolina—a school that George Pye LaRoche sent his youngest son, Cecil, to for help with his learning disabilities and his sometimes riotous behavior. Warren remembered Cecil as a kid with a few problems but mostly as just an inquisitive kid looking for the next big adventure, even if he had to make it.

One of his recurring adventures was trying to bring the most unique items to show and tell. A gaggle of hatchling geese didn't win him any high marks as they chased the teachers down the halls. And his antics with Dr. Kaczynski's car and the pond behind the school earned him an expulsion for the rest of the year. But the senior LaRoche took care of that with a generous five-figure donation to the school.

Cecil was different, and he was anything but normal. One of his proudest possessions was his 1982 World Champion Rodeo belt buckle. That belt buckle and pictures of him and his dad along with his longtime friends were the things Cecil cherished. And now he was gone…well, most of him anyway.

Warren snapped back to reality when Cookie McKee slid another beer in front of him.

"Where did that hog come from, Warren? I haven't seen hogs on Eddingsville Beach Road ever! I've hunted this whole island and never seen one," said Cookie.

"Well," said Warren thoughtfully, "game wardens have said they were coming; it was just a matter of time."

"Well, that's the craziest thing I've ever seen. And what was he doing in the middle of the road?"

"Don't know, but there was a pile of shelled corn he was eating when Bo hit him," said Warren cautiously. "And if you look, there was more corn just over the ditch."

"You think someone set this up? Like planned this?" asked Cookie.

Warren shrugged. "Don't know. How is he doing? Is he gonna to be alright?"

With a frown Cookie lamented, "He's knocked up pretty bad. Broke a rib and fractured his lower left leg. Good thing you didn't let him move. He could have made it worse or killed himself with that loose rib. He could have punctured a lung like that."

"Well, tell him I hope he gets better real soon." With that he got up to leave, and Cookie gave him a puzzled look.

"You not gonna finish your beer?"

"No thanks. I'm gonna go to the beach and think about some things," he said, and then he disappeared out the door.

As Warren left, driving north on Palmetto Boulevard in his old Chevy Blazer with the back window open so Pugzie could put his head out and around the side, he noticed the silver Range Rover pull out behind him. The windows were tinted dark, and he couldn't see inside the truck with the rear view mirror, but he knew it wasn't being driven by a local. The dark SUV was driving in the far right-hand lane of the four-lane road. Everyone that lived on Edisto drove in the center lane on the beach boulevard so they gained a split second in case a kid ran out in front of them. So he did what any Edistonian would do: he sped up and changed lanes to the outside lane too. About the seven-hundred block he turned into the beach access and turned his truck around to face the boulevard just in time to let the Land Rover pass by. This was a trick that locals used to aggravate the cops. They liked to play *Hill Street Blues* and follow people for no good reason. So everyone would find a way to turn the tables and then follow them. This one had worked for Warren before, and it did again. So now Warren and Pugzie were following the Land Rover. It turned on Mary Street and took a right on Jungle Road, heading for Highway 17. But at the last minute it turned into the entrance to the Waterfront Restaurant. Warren was smooth; he went past the entrance to the restaurant and turned into the exit. As he turned right again into the parking lot in front of the building, he was thinking he would be face to face with the Land Rover...but there was nothing there but the few parked cars of the early diners. He sat there puzzled for a moment and then drove out of the parking lot the wrong way through the entrance. He went straight across the street and turned around at the Sea Cow restaurant. This time he came back through the parking lot the right way—still no silver Land Rover. Befuddled and more than aggravated, Warren drove quickly down Jungle Road, took a right on 174, and headed straight to the Pavilion. He went quickly into the parking lot on the left side of the building and turned his truck so he was looking up Highway 174 and to the left looking down Palmetto Boulevard. If that Land Rover was going off the island, he would see it long before they saw him. Pugzie came up front and sat beside him on the other front seat. And so he and the big bulldog sat there for over an hour just watching for the silver SUV. It never came by on Palmetto Boulevard and never went on to the causeway from Jungle Road going out of town.

So Warren started the Blazer and drove slowly across the causeway that headed home. He didn't see the silver Land Rover pull out from under the old Wyndham Welcome Center building at the end of Jungle Road. It eased up to the stop sign at Jungle and 174 and just sat there until the old Blazer rounded the corner at the state park.

When he got home, he fed Pugzie and sat down at his dinner table with a ham sandwich and a notebook. He scrounged around and found a pencil. He started making notes about what happened and numbering them as to how important each one was to solving this crime. He woke up still sitting at the table, and Pugzie was growling at the door. It was 3:02 a.m. on the clock built into the stove. Warren didn't have a gun; he detested firearms. But he did have a baseball bat, and he had it in his hand when he swung the door open. The raccoon was as scared as he was and peed all the way down the steps as it ran for the woods. Warren chuckled and went bed.

About that same time, Moe Jurey was watching a fascinating scene through his night-vision rifle scope. He had been scouting for deer a little late that night and had come across somebody who apparently was trying to find something in Store Creek. They had invisible infrared lights shining on the water, so they certainly had an infrared night-vision device. They thought no one could see them. But Moe's Starlight scope was far more sophisticated, didn't use infrared light, and picked up the other lights right away as they blazed like headlights in his system. He could see them as clear as day and at two-hundred yards. They were only able to see about sixty yards. The person in the boat was easing along in a small inflatable dingy with something like a grappling hook on the end of a rope, which he kept throwing in the water. And they were towing another small inflatable raft about thirty feet behind them that had some kind of electronic gear on it. He could see several lights on the device light up, and when the green one came on, the person in the dingy would stop and try the grappling hook again several times. This went for about an hour and until Moe got tired of it. He took a deep breath and cut the rope holding the raft to the larger boat with the second muffled shot from his custom 300 Whisper rifle. The outgoing tide took the flashing equipment on the raft down the creek toward the river at an alarming rate. The person on the boat seemed to panic and tried to turn his boat around, but the tide and his small motor just wouldn't cooperate. By the time the mystery man was able to get going in the right direction, Moe had put a hole in the raft silently, and the raft began to list to the starboard side. A moving target at 220 yards, Moe was happy, so happy he put one in the inflatable dingy just at the water line on the bow. Now things got interesting as the late night prowler tried to figure out what to do.

Moe watched and chuckled quietly to himself as he eased down the tree he had been sitting in and went home. He didn't notice the old Datsun pickup camper parked in the woods there on Peters Point Road.

The next day crabbers found an inflatable dingy floating just under the water and hung up in their crab pot lines. It had one small hole in the bow, just at the waterline.

Chapter 19

Getting Somewhere?

Detective McKee was doing better. He was still in the hospital, but the doctor said he would be out in a few days and back to work in two weeks. The forensic reports and the trash information that Cappy was sending wasn't getting him anywhere. He needed to be back on the beach, working. Warren visited him several times and asked a lot of questions. Bo just blew him off and asked for more chocolate. But Warren was listening and learning more every day. He was thinking he might be getting somewhere. He wasn't sure, but it sure beat watching wrestling on the big screen at Whaley's Store.

Chapter 20

More Cecil

At the Sea Cow, Pale Dale Stall was trying to read the morning paper as Willy Wilkins kept talking about the latest news. Sweet William hadn't shown up at Whaley's for work, and his mother was calling everybody. It wasn't too unusual for William to run off. But he always called after the first day or so. And his mother was now in maximum panic.

Dale loved the grits and sausage gravy at the Sea Cow and treasured them when he had enough time to indulge his favorite. It certainly beat his usual generic Pop-Tarts.

Willy could talk about anything and nothing at all at the same time. He wasn't a bad guy, just another lonely Edistonian trying to connect with another human. He had been a big commercial realtor in Charlotte before the bottom fell out of the market. He luckily cashed out when the market was at the top. He took the money, traveled a bit, met a beautiful young woman, and built his Edisto dream home. It was always the first on the annual tour of homes. But he, like so many people that moved to Edisto, was lonely. His young lover was working on other things—real estate in a downward spiraling market.

Wanda, the woman he loved and admired, was not his wife. And no one asked why. She loved him for reasons only she knew and didn't share. She was working to make a name for herself in the local real estate market with Al Cabella and enjoying the challenge. The challenge, of course, was getting the sale and keeping the other realtors at arm's length. She was strong and self-assured, and many wondered about what the attraction to Willy was, but it was Edisto, and no one asked. But they all cared.

Pale Dale Hall was the best cabinet maker within two hundred miles, no lie. He handmade each one from scratch, the ornate cabinet that held the top-shelf liquors at Whaley's Store and the mantels and bookshelves for most of the upper-crust homes on Edisto. His work was the simple elegance that made for a classic piece of architectural-grade furniture. Ethan Allen in Charleston had nothing on him. But right now he wanted Willy to shut up before his grits got cold. He had a big job on Jeremy Cay and didn't want to be late or hungry when he got there. The cute, plump Latina maid, Serena, always tried to feed him. Today he wouldn't be lying when he said he had already had breakfast. But he knew she was looking for more than just someone to pamper. He had a girlfriend, Miss Penny, the love of his life, and intended to keep things that way.

Pale Dale drove the short distance to the house in Jeremy Cay. He was always impressed when he rounded the last turn to see the beautiful mansion. At over five-thousand square feet of bright beach and ocean colors, he felt like it was a masterpiece. It was owned by a quirky little Yankee guy named Lee Summerville. He had a woman too, Allie, his tall, slim girlfriend that he honestly admired if not loved. She was his live-in too. In reality, she really was just as smart as he, but she always let him think he was the one with all the brains. He liked being in charge, but he was also smart enough to know when to let her think she was in charge. It was a fair game that they played, and it worked well for their relationship. But honestly, without Allie he would be lost. And without Lee she would be lost.

Pale Dale was working on the kitchen cabinets while they were up north sailing their big boat back to Edisto. Each fall they would come down and stay in the big house. Each spring they would leave and rent it to the tourists. But this year the tourists were less likely to pay the price for a five-thousand-square-foot private estate home on a deep-water tidal creek, even if it came with a golf cart to use.

He had just started working and was high up on a ladder when he heard the screams. Through the open window he could see Serena, the maid, standing on the lawn by the boat lift with both hands on her face. She screamed again just as he got to her. Then, looking out the corner of her eye, she leaned back toward him so he could catch her as she faked the faint. But he had moved to get a better look at the latest arrival of Cecil. She hit the ground with a thud. The left arm made its entrance.

Chapter 21

A Trying Case

Boykin McKee was getting restless and wanted to get back to work. The sheriff called with the details of the latest find. But unlike the other arm, it had been ripped from the shoulder. It was doubtful that the injury was survivable. But again there was nothing new that would lead to the solution to what had become a very trying case.

Chapter 22

Becca's Life

The little black-haired girl could not remember when her mother had brought her to Edisto. But she was very young, about four or so. All of her days were spent being shuffled from one house to another, another place where someone took pity on her mother. They would take care of the little angel for the long hours while her mother toiled away. And work she did—every day, anywhere and everywhere. She worked heading shrimp, she shucked oysters, she washed dishes, and she shingled roofs. She was determined to get the money to send her daughter to a better school than what Edisto offered. The Edisto school was a small offering that Colleton County gave to Edisto Beach. It was the least they could do since the town of Edisto Beach gave Colleton County millions of dollars each year in taxes, almost half of the county's annual budget. They also gave them a small part-time library and a one fire engine department, but the most important things were the emergency medical personnel and the ambulance. The ambulance gave some small comfort to the old people that were waiting to die while living at Edisto Beach. But if you were real bad off, they called in the air ambulance. It came from Charleston. If you were in a life-or-death emergency, you wanted the air ambulance. It flew to a better hospital.

Every year as the first day of school came for the other kids, Becca's mother tallied up what she had saved. St. Paul's Academy was the closest and best in the area. If she got financial aid, she had enough to get the child through the third grade. Only nine more years to save for, but she would never make it. Just before Becca's first day of the first grade, her mother got sick, real sick. She couldn't stand up for the ten to twelve hours, and no one would hire her anymore. She had to move into an old trailer next to an old abandoned tomato-packing shed.

The shed came to life after dark each night. The night people made a lot of money making misery with their drugs. There was nothing her mother could do; it was all she could afford. After her first year at St Paul's Academy, it started to get worse. Her mother did the only thing she could do. She opened her home to less-desirable men who took advantage of her. They came and went and left cash behind. The men that came were from "off the island." Most treated her mother politely. Becca would bring them iced tea and answer their questions about school and her friends. She had no idea what her mother and these men talked about on those nights. She was always asleep when they left.

After her first year of school was over, her mother was so proud because she had done so well. She had someone drive them to Charleston, and they went to dinner at Red Lobster in Charleston. That night when the friend dropped them back home, they went inside and made hot chocolate with little marshmallows—her favorite. Her mother told her how proud she was of her "little angle." She kissed her softly on the head as she tucked her into bed. Becca was as happy as she had ever been. She had made her mom proud.

But later that night, right about 2:00 a.m., a big gray car pulled slowly into the yard. The drug makers had been gone. The driver got out and stumbled up the porch. No one locked their door, and he made use of that and quietly slipped into the back bedroom. Her mom screamed, and the visitor hit her to shut her up. He shut her up too good: the osteoporosis was worse in her back right at her neck, and it snapped cleanly and severed her spine. She was dead before she hit the floor. Becca was standing there looking at the old man when he turned to get out of the house after not finding a pulse.

The old man lunged at her as she scampered under the heavy dining room table, knocking over the Glade-scented bottle filled with a floral-smelling flammable liquid. It spilled and began to flow down the front of the table. She pushed back further under the table while kicking at him. He continued after her, screaming obscenities, throwing the chairs around the table out of the way. Just as he looked under the edge of the table, she hit him with the dustbuster that was still plugged in. It sparked as the wires tore loose from the unit. The flammable liquid had dripped onto his arms and back; they burst into flames. Apparently, he never learned what the firemen taught her in school: stop, drop, and roll.

He ran out the back door and stumbled against the old leaking drum that held the kerosene that fed the dilapidated heater. Knocking the drum off the stand, the contents spilled all over him. He created a bigger fireball that wasn't even human anymore. He ran to the packing shed looking for relief, but instead he slammed right into the vat containing the volatile chemicals used to refine the cocaine.

Becca watched in total amazement as the man as he ran outside. He looked like a burning marshmallow on the end of a stick. She ran to the back to the trailer that was already catching fire to get her mother out. But when she touched her wonderful, loving mother, she knew it was over and she was alone. All of the hopes and dreams they made were lying there in front of her, cold and dead.

She heard popping sounds from the packing shed and ran outside to see the fire jump across the trees to the other end of their home. The chemicals and bullets hidden in the shed ignited an even bigger fire, and it was getting really hot. She blindly backed away, shielding her face with her arms until she fell into the old drainage ditch. Suddenly, a flash of light and flames blew over her as she lay in the wet leaves lining the bottom of the ditch. It had all ended with one big explosion. When she looked up and over the edge, everything was gone—her home, her mother, and her life, all in one giant fireball. There was nothing but the trunks of the largest trees left standing.

Stuff was still falling from the sky as Becca went flying down the wire zip line her mother had helped her make to the creek and her secret hideaway. She hit the ground and ran for her special bag that held some crackers, candy, and a two bottles of water. It was the stuff she used when she went fishing at Steamboat Landing. She pulled the bag from out of the old hollow tree and ran. She had nowhere to go, but she knew there was an open boat shed at Steamboat Landing. She ran for what seemed like all night until she got to the landing. The boat shed was open, and there was a small skiff inside with the sail laid out to dry. She threw in her bag and climbed onto the boat and underneath the sail. She didn't realize that her climbing into the boat caused a rocking motion that made the dock line come loose. As she crawled under the sail, the line dropped off the dock and into the water. The little skiff gently began to ride out with the outgoing tide. She lay down in the bottom on top of the old life jackets and cried herself to sleep. The moon was bright and the creek was glassy smooth.

The little boat drifted as if guided by an old sailor's hand. It went out of Steamboat Creek, into north Edisto, and was heading for the open ocean beyond Deveaux Bank. Just when it looked like there was no stopping the little skiff's trek into the open waters of the Atlantic Ocean, the tide and wind changed. The bow swung around, and it headed back inshore. This time it was on the northern side of the waterway. And it followed the current right into Bohicket Creek and into the shallower water. The hand that guided the sleeping wayfarer brought it right between a forty-foot Albemarle cabin cruiser and a twenty-six-foot Regulator sport fisher. It stopped with a double thud against the two hulls. It was morning.

Chapter 23

Suzy Goes Walking

It was about dusk, days after the discovery of Cecil's other arm, and over on the St. Helena Sound side of Edisto Beach, Suzy Fontana was walking alone along the beach, just thinking about her kids that were with their dad for the weekend and about what she was going to do with the rest of her life. As she headed back to Bay Point Villas, where she always parked her "Mom Van," she opened the van door and stooped down to pick up a wayward plastic grocery bag that had blown across the parking lot and ended up next to her.

Her timing was impeccable. The door of the big blue Wyndham van parked next to her had quietly opened, and the large man that was going to grab her missed and tumbled out on top of her. Astonished at first, she rolled to the right, throwing him off balance, and started to laugh until she realized he wasn't one of her brothers or one their friends playing a joke.

The big guy lunged at her again, and she caught him with a Hannah Montana book bag right across his nose. It wasn't the homework that busted his nose, but the show-and-tell piece of petrified wood that caught the mark. You could see the pain in his eyes as the blood started down his face from a badly split nose. Not thinking, he put the cloth in his left hand against his bleeding nose, and his face took on a startled look. The pad was soaked in chloroform. And that's when Suzy realized exactly what was going on.

She jumped in the driver's seat and hit the ignition. This time the van cranked the first time. The left front wheel came across both her attacker's feet, and she could hear the bones crack as they gave way. She laughed at first as she sped away and then started to shake as she realized the outcome could have been very different. She swung into the deep underneath parking at Richard Stein's house, just a few blocks down from Yacht Club Road.

As she bounded up the stairs, Richard called out from behind his truck, "Hey, what's up?"

"Richie! Someone just tried to kidnap me!"

"Well, they would have brought you right back as soon as you started talking," he said.

"No, I'm serious! The guy had chloroform or something, and when I hit him in the nose, he put the cloth on his face to stop the bleeding, and I think he's just about knocked himself out."

"Are you serious?!" said the ex-Marine. "Hot dog, you just made my day, girl. Go upstairs and have Joyce call Cappy. I'll take care of this dude." With that, he produced his prized concealed-carry Kimber 1911 pistol and started running toward the Bay Point parking lot.

Just as he hit his top stride, the big blue van came around the parking lot, hitting the gate, bouncing off the curb, and heading straight toward him. Richie quickly let off two shots toward the engine and rolled into the myrtle bushes along the ditch. The van sped down Yacht Club Road and onto Palmetto Boulevard. He got out of the ditch and started running for the house to be sure it didn't stop there. It went right on by.

When he reached the top of the stairs, he saw that Joyce had Chief Cappy on the phone, trying to tell him about the attempted kidnapping. Suzy was looking real pissed off. Cappy was having a hard time understanding the excited woman. At the same time, she was having a hard time understanding him with a mouthful of Krispy Kreme doughnut.

So precious time went by, and the chloroformed driver of the van slowly came to his senses and began to focus on his driving and not on his nose or feet.

Police Chief Trent Crappy was sitting at the EZ Shop across from the Pavilion, where Palmetto Road turned left and became Highway 174, the only way on or off the beach. But by the time he was able to comprehend that an attempted kidnapper was escaping off the beach, the perpetrator was five cars ahead of him, as he pulled out of the gas station's parking lot, with a Moon Pie clenched between his teeth, to set up the road block.

So the villain drove casually to Live Oak Boat Landing further down the road to the state park, unencumbered by the lawman. Behind him, traffic had come to a standstill—coming and going. Edisto Beach was having its first traffic jam.

At the boat landing a man was waiting in a new Zodiac inflatable boat, idling in the current. The van hit the water without much splash, the door came open, and the dazed and confused wannabe kidnapper drifted with the outgoing tide to the boat. Even before he was securely inside the boat, the boat accelerated, planed out on top of the water, and headed for the South Edisto and points beyond.

Back on the beach, everyone was talking and asking questions. Angela Kromer tried to convince Cappy that the Wyndham van had already passed, but he was too busy looking at the bikini-clad drivers and putting his other deputies at the beginning of the causeway to pay her any attention. The roadblock came down several hours later after her brother, Andy from the Edistonian General Store, confirmed that the vehicle in question passed by long before the roadblock was set up.

Cappy started trying to get statements from those involved in the incident but wasn't getting very far. Bobby Hanson arrived and started getting the story right away. Warren and Pugzie wandered over from the Pavilion and stood against the wall and listened. They got more out of what was going on than anyone.

By the time it was all over, it was getting dark, and Warren had to use a flashlight to see the bubbles and oil coming from the sunken van at Live Oak boat landing. When he got Hanson over to the ramp, the bubbles were still coming up, and an oil slick was forming on the changing tide.

The next day the van was found and retrieved by the Charleston County sheriff's dive team, using about twenty people and six trucks. Julia Horton was there with her tow truck and had to wait only a few minutes on someone to give her the other end of the chain before she could start pulling it out. There were no bodies and no evidence, just two .45 holes in the front grill.

Cappy was standing there watching the truck come out, then turned to the man with the crew cut and said, "I could arrest you for discharging a weapon inside the town limits you know."

"Yeah, I know, but you won't." replied Stein.

But then Cappy thought better of it too.

Suzy gave a description of the assailant, but it was not much help. Julia came over to console her, but Suzy quickly perceived it as a come-on, when Julia invited her to come home with her and then to tried to kiss her.

Warren had been up all night with his pad and pencil. He had added several more items his list.

Chapter 24

William Wakes Up

Sweet William Richardson woke with a terrible headache. But his first immediate concern was the lower part of himself. He had been so very careful to always be protected during sex. Did the old camper guy wrap that thing? Did he take care not to be too rough on the old booty? As he slowly began to clear his head, he realized that it didn't feel as if he had been violated. And his nose told him that that was not his major concern right now. What was that smell? It finally registered, even though his eyes still could not focus. Pigs! "Oh my God!" he exclaimed. Suddenly he knew he was in much more trouble than he had imagined.

Laid out on his stomach, with his head hanging over the edge of a hard wooden table, he was just a few feet off the floor of a pigsty. He was not so comfortable. *I must be in a barn somewhere on the island,* he thought. But as he tried to look around, his view was limited by his ability to move his head. But the smell was not reassuring. He knew that if the pigs got him, the only thing that would be left would be his teeth. Pigs ate every part of a body. Even the teeth they ate would be damaged beyond recognition. Now he knew he was in really hot water. He began to struggle, but the more he pulled, the more he realized that he was bound with not just ropes but chains of various weights. Someone or someones wanted to be sure he stayed put. He started to panic and to cry like a little girl, like the little girl he always wished he had been. But after a long while, he realized there was no one listening to him. He thought of his dream of being a woman, a beautiful woman, a woman that both men and women wanted to be with, to hold, to cuddle, to love. He sank deeper into despair and began to sob.

So he began to sing. He sang the hymns from Trinity Church that he sang every week. He sang the rites of the Catholic church on Edisto, lovingly referred to as the "Church of the Holy Tool Shed" because it was a metal "Butler building" that really looked like an industrial factory building.

He had already relieved himself on the table and felt its warmth flow under his cool body. He was naked, and it was cool out, as if it were early evening. There were no bugs about, probably because the pigs stank so much.

He was also getting very thirsty, and the pains of hunger were starting to edge toward his consciousness. His last meal had been the Cream of Wheat his mother prepared for him that morning. At thirty-eight, he was still her little boy, and she made him breakfast every morning. Most of the time she didn't even know what day it was, and it really didn't matter. But her sole existence revolved around the ritual of Sweet William's breakfast. And…her reminding him that she was still his mother and demanding that he feel the guilt of her having not just birthed him over a forty-six-hour period but also sacrificed her whole life for his well-being.

"I just want you to know that when I get old and I'm about to die, I'm going to climb up on a volcano and throw myself in so you won't have to worry about burying me. I'll just go poof! And there'll be nothing but ashes floating away on the wind. No funeral home or grave, just gone and out of your life. No trouble would I be to you or anyone else.

"You'll never have to worry about all of the hours I toiled at the sewage plant just to put food on the table and to put clothes on your back. Yes, it was back-breaking work shoveling the sludge into the overflow pipe that took the raw sewage to the ocean. And yes, I was beaten by the town people if I put in too much shit at one time. But it was worth it to make sure you had the very best when you went to the Beach School. You would come home each night and tell me of all the things you learned about Bambi and Peter Pan. I was so proud. I just never knew you wanted to be Tinker Bell.

"But I still loved you. And I even took a second job working for Donald Cresset at the Sunset Grill, clearing off plates and preserving the leftovers. He would kick me when I didn't trim off the teeth marks on the fried flounder or if I didn't hide the wilted parts of the salad that I had to wash and re-serve."

Sweet William's family tree was a lot like a bamboo fishing pole—straight with a curve left at the end. But he was the exception to the rule. Queer as a plaid rabbit and extremely talented, he broke the mold in the Richardson family.

But none of that helped him in his present condition. The only thing that brought him any solace was the dripping water from the leaking roof. It came about every eight seconds, as he counted them, and he was able to turn his head so that it hit the crow's-feet wrinkle of his left eye and followed his nose, then ran straight into his mouth.

Not much, but it was something. He was alive, and that was all he had right now.

Chapter 25

William Wakes Up Again

Apparently William had fallen asleep. When he woke, he strained against his bindings, but there was no breaking or loosening of them. He finally relaxed and felt the chains shift a little. Somehow that had given him a little more room to move. He took advantage of it and shifted again. He felt one heavy chain fall away off the table he was bound to. He tightened again and shifted his weight to the right this time, and then he rolled as much as he could to the left. Again a chain released and fell away to the floor. But this time the pigs woke up. They stirred around and made a lot of noise and smells. They were still just several feet underneath the table he was laid out on.

He heard another sound—this one was human. It didn't speak, it just moved "human." He couldn't see who it was, but they moved slowly and deliberately behind him and close to his feet. He felt a hand touch his leg just above the ankle and move slowly up. Even in his terrified state, he became excited from the caresses. Then he felt the prick of a needle behind his knee. He panicked and screamed like that high-pitched little girl again. And his lights went out.

Chapter 26

Capt. Mikell

Captain Charles Mikell Savage was standing in the shadows watching as his captive struggled. He was getting restless knowing that the others might be getting closer to discovering his target. His real estate ploy had gained nothing. And trying to get information from Cecil didn't work because he had come apart, literally. He needed the information and needed it soon if he was going to beat the "commies and the rag heads." And now, according to someone he overheard talking to the old man with the dog, the Feds would be showing up soon. The sodium pentothal hadn't done anything but put his victim to sleep. Maybe he had given him too high of a dose. Well, this time it would be the lower end of the recommended dose. But if this didn't work, he would have to resort to more stressful measures. Water boarding worked in Iraq. He motioned for the shot to be given. As soon as the patient screamed and fainted, the captain rolled the gurney out of the pigsty. The old

Datsun truck had a small enclosed trailer attached to it, and the ambulance gurney's legs folded right up and locked into the cleats bolted to the floor. Calico Jack took a while to get in the small truck with his injured feet.

They drove without speaking.

The stolen safety harness and winch made it easy to lower the prisoner into the old fallout shelter. Although designed to lift a body out of a confined space in an emergency, it worked just as well at putting an unconscious one in one. As soon as Jack had the prisoner in and secured to the bed, the cover was replaced and locked from the outside this time. The brush used to hide the entrance was quickly replaced, and another leafy limb was used to brush the sand and cover the tracks to the truck and trailer. Ignoring the constant yelling and banging sounds, the captain climbed in the old camper and carefully drove around the circle driveway, staying off the shell sand so as not to leave any noticeable tracks. Alone.

Chapter 27

Dr. Hafez

Standing there contemplating his life, the distinguished older gentleman looked down and saw the ragged little dingy scratching against his boats. Never one to get upset, he just shook his head and walked down the plank to tie it off on the far side of his dock. He picked the bow line out of the water and was walking the line around the back of the Contender when he noticed the little bit of dark hair under the old dirty sail. He quickly pulled the boat up and jumped in. When he pulled back the sail, the little six-year-old girl jumped up, startled by the sunlight.

At first Becca thought it was the old man that she last saw on fire. But when she looked closely she saw the face of a kind man who seemed deeply worried.

She spoke first. "Are you OK?"

Befuddled by the question, he asked her the same one. "Are *you* OK?"

She looked around and said, "Uh huh."

She was dirty and smelled of smoke. He reached down and felt her forehead. She scratched her nose.

"Are you hurt?" he asked her in a soft, kind voice.

"No!" she said with an attitude as she rubbed her knee.

"Where did you come from?" She didn't answer. She just looked around. "Well, come on. We have to get you home."

"No," she said with a very low voice, shaking her head.

"Why?" She just looked away. "Well, come on. Let's at least get you cleaned up."

She stood up and lost her balance, and he caught her before she went overboard. She held on to his arm and didn't let go. He carefully lifted her and carried her up the long dock and into the house.

More like a hotel than a house, the dream home belonging to Dr. Saad Hafez and his wife, Michele, was built after he retired from teaching at The Medical University of South Carolina. They had no children of their own, and their relatives died in Iraq when Saddam Hussein used poison gas on the Kurds. Dr. Hafez had been at the medical school on an exchange program. It was a simple task for him to receive political asylum and continue his research on ovarian cancer. His wife was a small, pleasant lady who everyone in the Seabrook Island community loved. She had a close group of friends from all walks of life. They gave graciously to every noble cause but mostly to the Jenkins Orphanage for kids in Charleston. They hosted parties for the little ones on every holiday and an especially big one at Christmas. It brought a lot of joy to them both, until the little kids left. It was then that they felt the emptiness of not having their own.

Becca sat quietly while Dr. Hafez tended to her scratches. He carefully checked her over to be sure there was nothing requiring immediate medical attention. Michele was busy fixing food for the "little angel," more food than she could consume in a week. She ate without anyone saying a word. When she finished, she took her plate to the sink and started washing it, but Michele took over.

She was fascinated by her surroundings. There were many beautiful things, like pictures and statues and shiny globes you could see yourself in. She was like a new kitten that they just brought home. She went from room to room looking at everything, wide-eyed and awed. She went upstairs and stopped at the maid's small room and crawled up on the little single bed. Feeling safe and stuffed, she quickly fell asleep. Michele covered her with one of the small blankets that she knitted when they thought she may be pregnant. But yet again, the in vitro had not worked. They gave up that year. Both in their forties, they felt that they were now too old to give a newborn the best life.

They both silently walked downstairs and into the kitchen. The kitchen was their place. They spent most of their waking hours in the kitchen—Michele cooking and sewing and Saad conversing with other doctors about their research. They took their usual places when they had important subjects to discuss. He sat on the barstool across from the sink where she stood. He reached for the cordless phone, and she laid her hand across his.

He looked at her and could see the twinkle in her eyes. As is with two who have shared so much and lost so much, there was no need for words. He put the phone back into the cradle and held her hand in his. They both knew the consequences if they didn't report the found child. But hey, would it hurt to wait a few hours?

A few hours quickly turned into a few days and into even more years. There was never a report of a lost child in the area. And they watched every newscast for years. They did hear about the illicit drug factory explosion and that here were numerous unidentifiable bodies. (The drug people used the opportunity to off a few competitors and threw them in the mix.) They even heard about the woman and her child who both died in the explosion and fire. They each had separately driven to Edisto and snooped around, trying to get more information about the disaster and the death of the mother and small child. All they knew was that her name was Becca, and that was because she told them so.

So they kept the name added some k's to it, and concocted a story about her being the only relative who had escaped the Kurdish genocide. Her jet-black hair and dark skin made it all the more believable.

She grew quickly into a beautiful, smart young lady who never told her story. They didn't ask, and she didn't tell. It worked for everyone. She excelled in everything she did; she could focus like a laser on the task at hand. Her concentration came from pushing back her turbulent early childhood and the devastating pain of losing her beloved momma.

Time marched on, and her life was good. Her new parents loved her, and she loved and respected them. She was the model child. But deep inside there was turmoil brewing.

Bekka and her parents went to celebrate her first job after graduating from The Citadel. Now in the real world, she took the offer from Bank of America. They had gone to Charleston to celebrate at Meritage, a small tapas restaurant just off the Old Market. It was their favorite place. The atmosphere and decorations were a little Persian, and that made the Hafez family comfortable. It was a nice time, and they talked about Bekka moving to Charlotte to the bank's headquarters. They gave her a small peacock necklace, the Persian symbol of honor.

As they drove through the Holy City of Charleston, sadness about the upcoming separation slowly gave way to talking about the hope for her future and promises of visits back and forth.

Chapter 28

Wreck

Bekka's parents didn't indulge in drink, so that made the car crash even more devastating. Maybe if her fatefully found parents had been drinking and were a little more relaxed they wouldn't have died from the head-on collision. The young woman that hit them was surely relaxed and mostly uninjured. She reeked of alcohol and weed.

Bekka climbed out of the rear window of their car after she checked her parents and knew they were both dead. She checked the other driver and then made sure she was dead before she walked away from the cars. Others were quickly coming to help, but there was no need. She had taken care of everything.

She walked to a bus stop bench and sat down. She wanted to cry, but the tears wouldn't come. The big Red Lobster sign across the road stopped her tears—and triggered the suppressed rage she had been holding for years.

Chapter 29

Bekka's Next Trip

When Bekka was done washing the boat and covering it, she dressed casually and comfortably for her trip. She strolled past the white Prius and got behind the wheel of her black '99 Suburban. The little Prius hybrid allowed her to travel from Charlotte to Edisto quickly, economically, and unnoticed. The suburban was her personality. It was big and powerful yet comfortable and reassuring. She headed for Beaufort and friends who knew nothing of her exploits on Edisto.

Her position at Bank of America was secure, and she could come and go as she pleased. She was quickly promoted, and there was no limit to her income. She had a hefty $150,000 annual salary, and the assets left by her adoptive parents allowed her many pleasures and distractions. And right now Edisto was a distraction that was bringing her much pleasure.

But tonight she would be seeking more carnal pleasures with young men that had been locked up for weeks. She was headed for the night life of Port Royal near Parris Island and the Marine Corps Air Station. There she could trade her new backpack for something more volatile.

Chapter 30

Black Girl Love

The young Black girl did it for the respect and affection more than for the money.

He rolled off of her and panted like a race horse, then turned and gave her the smile she always cherished. "You're wonderful," he said

She smiled back and answered, "You ain't half bad either. Now get up so I can finish cleaning yo' house."

As she started to rise to get out of the big, fluffy bed, he grabbed her and kissed her passionately again, but she pushed him off playfully and hit him softly with the big, overstuffed pillow.

"Just a little more time?" he pleaded.

"OK, OK, but I really don't have enough time to do it again today. And yes, I know how you feel, and I know what you want. And you know it won't work on Edisto or anywhere else in the world."

"Well, if we moved to some isolated place, maybe we could at least try?" he suggested.

"How much more isolated can you be than Edisto, huh?" she said laughing. "Anyway, where on God's green earth do you think a sixty-year-old white man and a twenty-three-year-old Black girl could go and be accepted?" She paused thoughtfully and, in a soft, caring voice that he knew to be true, explained, "Yes, I care for you too. You know I do, but you have to remember this started as a business deal, and it's still a business deal. I have to clean your house. So don't go getting all soft and mushy on me now."

It didn't start out that way, but their relationship had grown into much more than Denique Miller had ever imagined. She was a single mom with one little three-year-old girl. She lived with her father and mother in Adams Run about twenty miles away. She worked cleaning the big houses on Edisto and went to Trident Tech two nights each week. She was smart, beautiful, hard-working, and falling in love with a rich, older white man.

Phillip Beal was a handsome and wealthy business man who lived on the one-hundred block facing the beach and the Atlantic Ocean. He was not very active in the social aspects of Edisto and became even more reclusive after his wife passed away two years earlier. Not much was known about him or his business.

It started one day when he came in unexpectedly and she was holding one of his deceased wife's dresses in front of her, swinging in front of the big full-length mirror in the bedroom. She was startled and embarrassed at first, but then he just laughed and told her to put it away when she was done with it.

She quickly put it back and made herself scarce as she finished cleaning the rest of the house. When she was done, she went into his office to apologize and get her usual hundred dollars for the cleaning. He was on the phone, walking across the wood floors that she took so much pride in maintaining. He was laughing, and she was afraid he might be telling someone what she had done. But she quickly realized that he must have made a big business deal and was bragging to one of his friends about it.

She liked watching him. She admired a man who had worked hard and made his own fortune. She knew he was generous because he gave to every cause that came his way. She respected him and his friends for what they did for the community. But now she was worried that it might all come to an end because of her little folly earlier with the dress. He put the phone down, and she braced herself for what was to come.

"So you like the dresses, Denique?"

"Yes, sir, and I'm sorry. I should not have touched her things."

"It's alright. They really need to go. It has been almost two years since she died. Maybe we should have a day of clearing out that stuff." She nodded affirmatively. "Would you like some of the dresses? They are about your size I would think." He spoke as he pulled out his roll of cash. "Maybe we should set a day and just do that, just move that stuff out of her closet and make some more room. What day could you help me?"

"What will you do with her things?"

"Donate them to an out-of-town church or some other distant charity. I don't really want to see them worn by any of the women of Edisto. They don't deserve them. And of course if there are any items you would like, you are more than welcome to them."

"Thank you, but I don't know if that would be appropriate."

"Sure it would. I would rather you have them than anyone else." So he handed her the folded bills and said, "Pick a day" in a rather dismissive way.

Chapter 31

Out with the Old

A few weeks later she arrived on the agreed Monday morning at 10:00 a.m. to go through his deceased wife's things. He met her at the door unshaven, dressed down, reeking of alcohol, and with a certain resolute manner that she had never seen before. They walked straight into the bedroom. He had already been at work most of the previous night. All of the dresses were on the floor, and her shoes in their tidy boxes were pushed off to one side. Her lingerie and undergarments where thrown haphazardly in a box that was overflowing. He began to bark orders at her as if she were no more than his slave. She didn't like it.

"Get those things out of here. Take them away, anywhere I don't care, just get them out of my sight."

"Yes, sir, I'll take them down the elevator and put them in your truck."

"Yeah, put them in my truck. Here are the keys. Drive them to the bridge and throw them in, all of them."

She was seeing a side of him she had never seen before. He was hurting, and she didn't know what to do except exactly what he said. She quickly and quietly moved all of the things into the truck and, without saying a word, drove off from the big beach house. She didn't know where she was going, but she just needed to get the things away from him. She realized that many of the items where valuable and decided, *Why not make some extra cash?* So she drove to her home in Adams Run and opened up the old barn behind the house. There were old tables along the sides, and she took the clothes and placed them on newspapers that covered the dusty tops. She then took the time to neatly fold each piece and sort them into stacks. One stack was for the consignment shop, a small one was for the charity shop, and the last and the largest was for her to consider keeping for herself. Most of the shoes fit, and she decided she would keep all of them for now. Pleased with herself and realizing she had been gone for almost two hours, she jumped in his truck and headed back to Edisto.

Chapter 32

Bailey Island and More Cecil

A select few members of the Edisto Perseverance Association were meeting in secret out on Bailey Island. These were people from the beach that sought to benefit from the development of the island by pretending to "save it" from development. But the face on the wide-screen TV of the biggest developer this side of hell told a different story. Dell Dread was the creator of large tracks of residential areas along the Atlantic coast. His communities were known as "house farms" and his motto was, "I never met a tree that couldn't be better used by getting out of the way and making lumber to build a house." His gaudy designs stacked houses so close together that the neighbors could reach out of their windows to borrow a cup of sugar. Shoddy construction and cost overruns were his specialty. And these people knew it and had invested heavily into it. As David Canton put it, "We are laying the groundwork for someone else to worry about saving Edisto and making a killing looking like saviors."

Dread spoke of all of the money that they would each have, just as soon as he had all of the deeds and permits in hand to start construction. He never mentioned the sprawl or traffic that would paralyze the small community. And they didn't care, because each of them knew they would have to leave Edisto soon to be closer to better geriatric health-care facilities. They were selling the soul of Edisto to add a few more years to their miserable lives.

But misery loves company, and it had just come callin' with a scream that came from the end of the long dock that went out across the marsh and into Bailey Creek. The old farts "ran" (or made their way as quickly as they could) to find out what the ruckus was all about. When they collectively arrived out of breath at the end of the dock, they found Mrs. Henrietta Stone pale and shaking. She was pointing at the incoming tide with her eyes closed. But there was nothing there. Ernie Bonson, a town council man, shook her back to reality, and she thanked him with a roundhouse that came across his left ear.

"What did you do that for, you old coot?" he said, surprised by her strength and reeling from the pain and ringing inside side his head.

"What the hell are you shaking a seventy-eight-year-old woman for, you pompous ass?" the old lady yelled.

"I was trying to bring you back to your senses. You were screaming like a banshee!"

"Well, never mind me. Get that body out of the creek, you moron.

"What body? There's nothing there," said Bonson.

Mrs. Henrietta looked at the dark, flowing water with surprise. "Well, it was right there, tumbling along the creek bed."

"Are you sure?" asked another "preservationist."

She was contemplating pushing the old fart in the creek when she saw it roll by again. "There it is!" They all turned to look, and each saw a glimpse of a foot pass just below the surface. Bill Skatell, the president of the Edisto Perseverance Association, fainted after screaming like a little girl and fell backwards into the pluff mud of the tidal creek.

So the county dive team came back to Edisto later that day and pulled out more of Cecil LaRoche, which they didn't mind at all. On the way in they stopped at Martin's Market for breakfast, and on the way out they stopped at Po Pigs for a barbeque lunch. "A perfect day!" the lead detective said. "Found what we were looking for and ate food as good as Momma makes."

The coroner called Sheriff Mallory and told him the good news: Cecil was definitely dead. He could not possibly be alive with this much missing.

"Looks like he was separated."

"Separated from what, his wife?" asked the sheriff.

"No, the rest of his body, of course."

"I believe that he was torn apart. It looks like all of his legs and arms were tied off in separate directions and then pulled. He came apart like a wishbone. So far we have his right and left arm and the left leg and torso. We are missing a leg and his head. I'll need to run more test to confirm they match, of course."

"No, you don't need to run any test. He's dead. What more could a test tell you? NO! Don't answer that. Just put it with the rest of him in the freezer, and label it good."

Chapter 33

Denique Takes Care of Beal

Denique arrived back at Mr. Beal's house just before 4:00 and quickly ran up the stairs and into the unlocked rear door. She was heading for the bedroom when she realized he was sprawled out on the leather sofa that overlooked the dunes and the beach. She saw that he was asleep, so she went into the bedroom and began cleaning and reorganizing the closets and drawers. When she was done, the sun was setting, and she walked into the great room and stood behind the couch where he was lying. She had never seen the sunset from that view and was instantly mesmerized by its beauty.

He moved slightly and opened one eye to look at her. She could tell he was not feeling so well. So with no school that night, she decided to play cook too. She first made a pot of coffee and took him a big mug. He looked at her in disbelief, and it almost seemed a look of protest. But then he relaxed, and she helped him sit up.

"Are you alright, Mr. Beal? You look a little pale."

"Yeah, no, I'm not alright. I'm mad and pissed off."

"Did I do something wrong?"

"No. NO, not at you! I'm mad at Betty. Betty, who I bought everything she ever dreamed she wanted for and gave her everything that she even hinted at. And what did she do for me? Nothing, not a damn thing. Thirty-six years of trying to make her happy, and all I ever wanted was a little bit of love and affection. I mean, come on. She had time for all of her charitable work and all of her bridge club friends but not a minute for me, not even a second. God, I know it's wrong, but I'm so glad she's gone. And I feel so guilty about it."

His eyes teared up, and she was astonished at the emotion that flowed from this man. She didn't know what to do, but she wanted to help. So she moved to the ottoman in front of him and sat down and looked at him. She cared for this old white guy, and she didn't know why.

He looked into her deep black eyes and felt that there was a place to lay his burden. And he did. He started from when they were in college and dating, and everyone said they made such a great couple. Then there were the families that decided they should marry, and they did. It was like a blizzard to him at the time. Her father brought him into the import business, and he took to it right away. Then her father died, and he was left in charge.

But she wanted all of the things that Denique took away in the truck. And he was obliged to provide them for her. He talked for over an hour, letting it all flow forth. When he was done, he sat up straight and said, "WOW, I feel so much better!"

Denique smiled and said, "Let me take care of you for a while."

Puzzled, he just looked at her. She rose quickly and, with a determined stride, went into the master bedroom and started the shower.

She laid out his shaving things on the counter and returned to him. Without a word she led him into the ornate bathroom and helped him undress. He was not embarrassed, and she did not stare. He stepped into the shower and felt the hot water bring him back to the world of the living. He washed quickly, wondering what was next. She breezed into the room with a big towel, and he stepped out into a warm towel she had heated in the dryer for him. He smiled and began to dry off. When he walked into the bedroom, she had laid out his favorite clothes—an old pair of Levi's and a flannel shirt. He quickly dressed because he could hear her in the kitchen, and the suspense was driving him wild. He stepped out into the smell of shrimp, butter, and garlic. He knew it was shrimp and grits. He sat down at the counter.

They had not spoken a word since he got up from the couch. He was numb with anxiety, waiting for what was next.

She turned from the stove with the steaming plate and said, "Momma makes the best, but mine ain't bad."

"It smells delicious! I didn't know you could cook, but then I never asked you, did I?"

"Every Black woman can cook, some just better than the others."

"I really don't know anything about you or your family. I don't even know your daughter's name"

"Jasmine, but we call her Jazz cause she likes music so much."

He ate slowly, scared she would leave. He listened intently to her every word. And when she finished telling him of her life and he had finished his dinner, they washed up the dishes and he stood beside her, dried them, and put them away.

With the kitchen chores done, she immediately gathered her things and headed for the door. He was right behind her.

"Denique, do you have to go? I mean, it's not that late. You could stay and we could talk."

"I'm sorry, Mr. Beal, but I have another house to clean in the morning and classes after that, so I have to go."

His mind raced with excuses for her to stay, even if just a little longer, but he held them to himself. She opened the door and turned, and he reached in his pocket for his money, but it wasn't there.

She looked at him warmly and said, "It's on your night stand," and she reached up and kissed him on the cheek.

He blushed and said, "Come back tomorrow, and I'll pay you for what you've done."

She stopped about halfway down the steps and said, "I'll call when I can come clean for you again."

Chapter 34

Lunch

The next time she came to clean, it had been almost two weeks since she had seen him. He called, but she put him off knowing that things were coming to a head in their relationship. He was there and opened the door for her when she arrived. He tried to start a conversation about minor things, but she was busy cleaning and kept moving away and into other rooms, not ignoring him, just getting on with her work. Finally, about 11:30, he caught her in the third-floor laundry room.

"It's lunch time. Where do you want to go?"

"What? We can't go to lunch together! My Lord! Can't you hear them women of the beach? 'Mr. Beal done took up with that little Black girl who cleans for him.' No, none of us need to start that."

"No, I insist. I took the liberty of buying you a dress. I think it will fit, and it's close to the one you were holding in front of yourself that day." He popped it out of a box he had hidden behind himself. It was a stunningly beautiful dress, casual but elegant in a timeless way. Her eyes grew wide at the site of it, and it was her exact size. "Now come on. Let's go!" he said with a big smile.

"No, this is not a good idea."

"Sure it is. Were just talking like old friends."

"Right, white and Black, sixty-something and twenty-something. Yeah, just chatting about things we have in common. Mr. Beal, I can't do this."

"Why not?"

"Like I told you, people will talk."

"Let them."

"No, you don't understand. Some of these old ladies are other clients of mine. I clean their houses too."

"Please, Denique, please. I'll pay you extra."

"How much?"

"I don't know, a hundred dollars?"

"And you buyin'? Let me put this on."

So off to the Plantation Grill for a nice, relaxing lunch they headed. She was impressed with the Cadillac and mentioned it several times. When they entered the restaurant, all eyes turned to them.

"See, I told you," she whispered.

"I don't care," he answered.

"Well I do"

"Why?"

"Cause I don't want them talking bad about you," she said more urgently.

"And I don't care," he replied and smiled joyfully.

They sat on the side next to the big picture window, looking out over the golf course. It was a wonderful lunch, and they talked quietly about her life and family. But she felt uneasy because she could feel the others watching and whispering. They finished a wonderful meal and headed for the door. Just as they were about to go out, the manager stepped out of his office and said, “Mr. Beal, how good to see you again.”

Beal turned and responded, “Nice to see you too, Eric.”

“I was wondering if I could have a quick word with you about a small matter,” he said with a fake smile, “in private. It will only take a minute.”

Beal, in his naivety, replied, “Sure. Denique, would you excuse us?”

The hairs on her arms were tingling. She knew what was coming.

“Sure, I’ll wait in the car.” She almost blew him a kiss but thought better of it.

As they stepped into the office, Eric wheeled around and almost spat out the words. “What the hell are you doing, Beal? You can’t walk in her with her. Have you lost your ever-loving mind? You hadn’t gotten seated before other people in the restaurant started texting me about the old man and his young Black girlfriend.”

“Well, I didn’t see anyone walk out.”

“They wouldn’t dare; it’s Edisto. They will just never come back into this restaurant.”

“And neither will I, Eric. Oh, and by the way tell your boss, Lee, I’m calling in his note. He has till the end of the month to deliver my $160,000 the same way he got it—in cash.”

The young buck went pale, and the wind dropped from his sail. He collapsed against his desk. He struggled to speak, but the words wouldn’t come. He knew his career had just ended. Lee Vern, the owner of the Plantation Grill, would destroy him. He knew that he had just committed employment suicide. Beal had always funded Vern when he ran out of money or luck. And Eric had just closed his boss’s bank.

Outside, she almost ran out of the restaurant for the Cadillac. When she got there, she just stood fuming and looking across at the white women playing tennis.

"Serena would kick all of your butts left-handed," she hissed.

He came up from behind and started to open the door for her, and she brushed past him to let herself in. They drove back slowly, with her reminding him that it was a bad idea.

He just smiled and was glad to have her with him, even if she was pissed off and he would never return to his favorite restaurant.

Back at the house she immediately changed and went back to work cleaning the kitchen. He walked in and took out his roll of cash and left four hundred-dollar bills on the counter in front of her. Startled, she turned to face him with a look of disbelief.

"What, you think you can buy me?"

Stunned, he replied, "No! Never would I imply that I was buying you."

"Yeah, you better not even think that. Slavery went out a long time ago, mister."

"I can give you money if I want to."

"Sure, but what do you want for that money, eh?" she said with a scowled look.

"To talk to you? To be with you? To share some things with you?" he pleaded.

"Look," she said, finally letting down her defenses and relaxing a little. "I really like you, Mr. Beal. But we cannot have a relationship. Maybe a friendship, but even that's gonna be a stretch," she said resolutely.

"Well, let's try. I want you to start coming twice a week from now on."

"And what do I do when I get here? You're not really a very messy person," she grumbled at him.

"We talk and maybe go to lunch again."

"NO! No lunches or dinners or anything else like that. We stay here," she said emphatically.

"OK. So when can we start?" he said, smiling.

"Start talking?" she began to relax.

"Yeah, just sit and chat."

"I got it. You talk while I clean," she smiled.

And so they did. Pretty soon he was helping with the cleaning, and not long after, he would clean the house before she arrived. It was a sweet arrangement, and it was working for both of them until Denique started to sit closer to him on the couch when they watched TV. Her love life was pretty much nonexistent.

Chapter 35

Beal's Folly

Denique and some of her friends would go out to the local clubs, but they were not for her. The young men were always drunk, wanting to fight, and were disrespectful of all of the women. So she just quit going. She began to feel even more relaxed and comfortable with Mr. Beal. She looked forward to their time together, and both of them were getting what they needed: love, respect, and tenderness.

They crossed the line the day he pulled his shoulder moving the freezer. She had had a bad day with some young kid hollering at her saying he wanted to spend some time with her. "I wants to get to know you, like real deep." It was someone she had never seen before.

Beal was laid out on the big bed with only his shorts and T-shirt on, moaning like a baby when she came in. She asked what happened and started messaging the muscles that he strained. He tried to make it sound heroic, but it didn't work. She went to the bathroom and came back with steaming hot towels. She worked the sore muscles, and before long she was getting a massage too. That was a blissful year ago.

Now she was staring at the blasted and burned-out remains of his cherished Cadillac sitting under the McKinley Washington Bridge. They removed the charred body and most of the cocaine that didn't ignite when the car exploded.

Her heart sank into the deepest pit of her soul. She thought that this was a good and decent man. How could she have missed that he was just a sorry-ass drug dealer.

Detective McKee walked over and asked, "You two were pretty close, eh?"

"Huh? What do you mean?" she asked, puzzled by his brash inquiry.

"I mean you loved him, didn't you?"

"Nah, that white man? No way. I just cleaned his house." She knew he could tell she was lying.

"There's no need to ask you any questions about this. But I'm sure you have some."

"No, I got no questions," she replied, looking down at the ground.

"OK, I'll be over there in my car writing up the report if you think of any."

"No, no questions," she said, and she started to sob quietly.

So he walked back toward his car but made a stop by the evidence van. He asked if there were any indications of how someone could blow up this respectable citizen from their point of view. A rather geeky Asian-looking fellow with thick glasses looked up and handed him a small tagged evidence bag. The sheriff's department ID tag around his neck said "Lucas Rookus."

"Tannerite. Generally used by gun nuts to blow up junk and impress their friends. Very new and very dangerous stuff. I don't know how anyone could have thought this through. They must have really hated this guy to spend all of the time it would take to plot this murder."

"Why, what is Tannerite?" inquired Bo.

Peering over his glasses he said, "Two harmless powders that are mixed together that ignite when shot with a high-powered rifle. Ammonium nitrate and aluminum powder combined in the proper amounts make an explosive that is stable when subjected to less severe forces than a high-velocity bullet impact, such as a hammer blow, being dropped, or impact from a low-velocity bullet or shotgun blast. It is also not flammable; an explosion cannot be created by a burning fuse or electricity. Because it is sold as two separate powders rather than as the combined mixture, it is even more stable and easier to transport. It's sold in many places without the legal restrictions that apply to other types of explosives."

"Why would it be so hard to blow up this guy's car with the stuff? Sounds like you just set it under the car and shoot it," he said with a shrug.

"Ah, yes, detective, but how do you just set a twenty-pound package about the size of a brick under someone's car without them noticing? And how do you make sure they park exactly over it? The charge was close to the driver's seat under the hood of the car when it went off. It launched the motor like a rocket over one hundred feet over there and into the marsh in one direction, and the rest of the car from behind the windshield was thrown under the bridge."

"So…?" he asked.

"So they didn't know what they had or how to use it properly," the geek explained, getting a little testy.

"How'd they set it off? You say they shot it with a high-powered rifle?"

"Haven't found any evidence of the bullet, casing, or rifle. Just the traces of Tannerite all over the place, but I'll bet the stuff was hooked to the car close to the fuel line. The charge was most likely bolted up underneath somehow, and they managed to get him to park where they had a clear shot. Your killer was not too far away and knew where to shoot the car to detonate the package. This was a well-thought-out and probably rehearsed killing."

"Wow. OK, thanks for the info," he murmured and shuddered as he walked away.

As soon as he closed the door of his car, he heard her sniffle. She was in the back seat slumped down and looking very lost and hurt. He turned the rear-view mirror so he could see her. She was beautiful and broken right now.

"Mr. McKee, what happened to him? I mean, he was such a nice guy. What was he doin' with all that coke?"

"It looks like he had been in the drug running business on the outside, looking in for years. Told everyone he made his money importing and day trading in the stock market, when he was actually responsible for bringing in loads of drugs every month. We would catch the little guys but never could find the big guy making the deals and setting up the shipments. Apparently, he had a one come in, and his normal system of delivery must have been down, so he decided to handle it himself."

"Who killed him, Mr. McKee?" she asked.

"I don't know, but I'll bet it was the same person that messed up his normal delivery. They may have set him up for this." After a brief silence he asked, "You OK?"

She didn't answer; she just sat with her face in her hands, sobbing quietly.

He got out of the cruiser, walked back over to the ambulance, and looked inside. There was nothing to see as the remains of the former Mr. Beal were zipped up tight in a distorted black plastic body bag. He nodded to the EMS attendants and walked back to the remains of the car. Just as he stepped onto the grass from the paved parking lot, he felt something under his foot. At first he didn't see what it was, but when he looked closer, he realized it was a knife. A funny-shaped knife with a down-turned blade. He called to the geek in the evidence van and motioned for him to come over.

Lucas Rookus strolled over and looked down. At first he didn't see it, but then he smiled real big, reached into his coat, and pulled out an evidence bag. He carefully lifted it from the grass with his gloved hand and placed it in the bag.

"A shafra!" he said with excited amazement. "The knife of the Persians. Used in ceremonies and tribal rituals. Very rare. Wonder what it's doing out here on a coastal sea island, eh?"

"Do what? What are you going on about?" asked the dumbfounded detective.

"This is a rare knife, and it hasn't been out here long. I would dare say the perpetrator dropped it, or it was in the car."

Bo thought for a moment, then asked, "Were there any stab wounds or cuts on the body?"

"I'll go look!" said the now-excited geek.

Bo continued to look around the area for other signs and evidence. Shortly after the geek came back without the knife and was smiling he said, "His throat was cut."

"With that knife?"

"Don't know until I test for blood on it. But my bet is that if there is, it's a match and that your killer is a rag head."

"What the hell is a rag head?"

"Arab, Persian, someone from the Middle Eastern countries who wears a turban," he said smiling broadly.

"Really, you got this figured out, eh?"

"No! I mean no, sir. I mean, it could be that there is a Middle East connection here: the knife, the use of a bomb..." he explained excitedly.

Bo looked back at his car and watched Denique slip out and move slowly to join the other gawkers.

"So we now have Middle Eastern drug dealers? That's a bit of a stretch, don't you think?" He smiled but was not amused.

"No, I think you have a Middle Eastern murderer." He sneered back at the shocked detective and spun on his heel to return to his van.

The detective looked puzzled at the remnants of the car, then turned and watched as the small, dark feminine figure blended into the crowd. He shook his head and walked slowly and thoughtfully back to his car.

The big, powerful black boat motored past the scene with the same interest as the other boats, but only the dark-haired captain of the sleek Contender was all smiles as she slid the Weatherby 300 high-powered rifle into the floor locker of the boat.

It had taken her quite a while to plan out the end of Mr. Beal. She crawled under the car one night at The Sea Cow restaurant and worked for almost an hour drilling and bolting the metal canister to the firewall behind the engine. She even endured his small talk with his other male friends about how easy women were around Charleston. But the biggest insult was when he relieved himself just before he went back inside the restaurant, and it puddled under her left shoulder. But now that score was settled too. All that was left was to dispose of his delivery man's body.

Chapter 36

Mayor

Jake McFee, who had been the mayor of Edisto Beach forever, waddled into town hall and on into his office. His "Jake leg" was hurting him bad, the result of a cold front and his wife having shot him in the ass years before when she found him in a compromising situation at her father's furniture store. Jake had been the mayor of Edisto for more than twenty years and was not about to quit now. (Although most voters thought he should.) No one wanted the job; it didn't pay but $800 a year. But Jake wanted to keep it so he didn't have to stay home and listen to his wife. So no one ran against him in the past five elections because they understood his predicament and felt sorry for him (and her).

Suddenly, he noticed everyone heading for the back door. It was an emergency! There was no way he could move fast enough to get out with them, not with his aching leg. He was trapped! The bane of his existence came strolling around the corner and stood right in the doorway.

"Well, what you gonna do about this murderer on the loose?" asked Neuron Fornsby. "I think Pete Alexander is involved in it. You know, Pete and Cecil were good friends and business partners at one time. But I hear they had a falling out. I think you should bring in Pete for questioning. I could help, you know. I've seen how they do it on that NCIS show. Let me do it. I'll have a confession out o' him in no time flat and solve this case in twenty-four hours. What do say, Jake?"

"Neuron, what are you doing here?"

"Oh, Susan told me to get out of the house and not come back until after lunch. So I got the time!"

Jake shook his head and said, "Go home, Neuron, or at least somewhere else."

"Oh come on, Jake. Give me a shot."

"NO, Neuron, leave! I've got my own to work to do. I've been working for years on stopping that water line from Charleston. Next thing you know they'll have good, drinkable water and want city sewer service, and this whole damn place will be another Las Vegas. And by God I alone have to stop all of it if I'm going to keep this community stuck in the 1950s."

"Well, can I ride in the police car with Chief Cappy today?" asked the large-nosed one.

"Sure, just get outta here!"

Neuron shuffled quickly out the front door, yelling for Chief Cappy to stop the police car, but he was driving as fast as he could to escape a fate worse than death. All of the town employees and visitors came back in through the back door. They settled back into their routine of gossip and reading trashy novels, all except for the one strange woman who had strolled in and picked up a map provided by the Edisto Beach Police Department. It was a map of the beach and all of the beach accesses. She smiled politely to the ladies in the front office and went out the door with her treasure. Several guys in the building department noticed her a little more cause she was so easy on the eyes, her long black hair shifting in the breeze. But they figured she was just another tourist on vacation, another passing beauty. She opened the door of her Prius, took out a camera, snapped several pictures quickly of the town complex, slid in behind the wheel, and drove off in her quiet hybrid car.

Chapter 37

Boxes All Around

As Warren sat there in Coots Lounge, contemplating what he knew and what he thought he knew, the beer started to loosen the little gray cells. Random ideas and thoughts started to gel and become possibilities. Some were silly like aliens and Miss Mary's voodoo. But others, like both Sweet William having gone missing and the recent explosion of the drug-laden Cadillac, were possibly more than coincidence.

The crazy Scotsman, Campbell McCray, came in hollering and carrying on about the latest insult to his intelligence. He was noisily complaining about the new fixtures on the local power poles. Being the only "certified town electrician," he climbed the local poles, replacing the street-light bulbs regularly. Apparently, the electric utility company had been installing some new device on some of the poles, and they were in the way when McCray went to change the bulbs. But they were haphazardly placed on the poles. None of them were in the same place on the poles. He had come to Coot's to complain about having to work around them...and for several shots of Jameson Irish Whiskey.

"Who's the rocket scientist that came up with that idea?" he blared in his Scottish accent. "And what the devil do they do? Get in my way, that's what they do!"

Well, Warren decided that he should go look for those boxes and get out before a conversation got started that would keep him there for hours; and he didn't have anything going on anyway, so why not? He liked to just drive around Edisto with Pugzie and watch the sunsets and look at the people. It was his way of relaxing. And sure enough, after checking around, he found the funny boxes that appeared on six telephone poles all over the beach around Bay Point. He wondered what they were and decided to try to find out exactly what they did. Richard Stein had a cherry picker elevated lift just a few yards down the street from one, and he decided he was going to get it later.

About midnight, Richie's cherry picker was underneath one of the boxes at Bay Point Villas, and Warren was looking for wires. There were none. Baffled, he just pulled hard and brought it down. Noticing that there was a hole and something that resembled a lens, he quickly shoved it into to a paper grocery bag and climbed down. He pushed the cherry picker back the short distance he had moved it and went straight home so as to get at the box.

Once inside his house, he closed the curtain to the one window in the kitchen and took the box out of the bag, keeping the end with the hole pointed at the desk light to blind it if it was a camera. Then he started removing the screws. He had to pry the box open after he removed the screws because it was also sealed with silicone, apparently to keep out the moisture. There were lots of circuit boards, lights, batteries and a small camera with a big lens inside. He pulled out the batteries, and all of the glowing lights went out. There were parts of what looked like a cell phone too. There was also another section of the box with a silver tube in it and a dial that had the word "roentgens" on it. Warren remembered the word from his army days. That meant it was a Geiger counter. Why a Geiger counter? There was nothing radioactive on Edisto or anywhere around. Or was there?

Warren sat down and started to think real hard. It took a while but it finally came to him.

Chapter 38

Warren's Life

Warren had been single for a long time, about seven years now. He had a woman in his life for a while, and things went pretty good for the first few years. He was teaching military history at The Citadel. They met in Charleston at the Chocolate Affair, a fundraiser for The Friends of the Jenkins Orphanage, and they magically hit it off in a big way. After that night, they spent a lot of time together, just enjoying being with each other like most "head over heel" newfound loves. Mostly, they went to other social functions and dinners and highbrow performances.

Once, when they had gone shopping for a birthday present for Warren's niece in Charleston, they stopped at the fountain in Tanger Mall. They started throwing money in the fountain and making wishes that they would divulge to each other only with hints, raised brows, and wry smiles. Warren threw in a quarter. She threw in two. Another throw from Warren and in went his dollar that floated across the surface. She threw in a five and smirked, then shook her head no as she watched him. He carefully folded the one hundred dollar bill into a small paper airplane and gingerly tossed it towards the fountain. She looked amazed at the site as it slowly circled the water falling from the tall statue in the middle. They were both beginning to feel excited by the contest. It seemed as if it was going to hang in the air forever.

It was only ended with the splash of a kid as he jumped in the fountain, grabbed the expensive airplane, and ran away. "Hey, that's my dream, you little shit," Warren shouted, as he ran down the hall to recapture his passionate hopes for the evening. Eventually, he gave up, and as he was walking back to her, he smiled and remembered the money in the fountain went toward the Jenkins Orphanage.

They married and lived west of the Ashley along the river. They never had any children.

But as with all good things, this one had to come to an end—the passion faded, and her love for him died as well. Something went wrong, and Warren never really knew what it was. She started looking for answers to "life's persistent questions" in the bottom of a bottle. Every day she was sure it was bound to be in the next quart of ol' Heaven Hill bourbon.

She died in her sleep everyone was told. But drunk and a pillow over her face—there came an end to the constant beatings and terrible words he endured for all those years.

Right after her death and for weeks to come, the ladies from the Catholic church, The Church of the Rolled (Rolling) Stone, would stop by with their casseroles and covered dishes and condolences. They never knew the pain of loving someone who hated you. They never knew the torture of the words that cut like a knife into his soul every night. And now they had no idea of his joy and relief after her passing. He hid it well.

The day after her funeral, they came and weeded the flower beds in front of the house, all the while proclaiming what a wonderful gardener she was. So he scattered grass seed and thistles in between their newly planted flowers. They even planted the small garden off to the left side of the backyard as a memorial to her service to the community and the Jenkins Orphanage. He caught caterpillars and beetles and set them free in the garden to eat the plants. He sat on his porch speechless and stunned by their ignorance of his release from pain as they worked tirelessly to make his life more beautiful and a little more pleasant. Each day when they left, he pulled out his own bottle and contemplated his next attack on the flower beds and garden they gave him.

For weeks they came. They would all speak of her "saintliness" and the good she had done for everyone. These women never saw the beatings she gave him and the mental abuse he had endured for oh those many years. All the while she sang in the choir and presided over the school auction. That most wonderful woman of church and school took pride in not leaving a visible mark on his wounded body or his tortured soul.

But Pugzie saved him. He came when Warren needed him most, a small, little puppy sitting on the side of the road. Warren moved to Edisto to do as many others do, to hide and forget. And they were inseparable. If Warren went to the Pig or rarely to church, Pugzie accompanied him, sat by the door, and patiently waited for his friend to emerge. If only the dog were a woman…

Chapter 39

Calico Jack

Calico Jack looked at his patient, hostage, guest through the eyes of a plaid rabbit and smiled, even though his own feet hurt like hell.

This time when Sweet William woke he was very cold and not alone. There was another person in the room. He was different, but more like Sweet William than he knew, and his ankle wasn't chained to a metal bed.

Calico Jack had become a victim of his own greed. Now he, too, was a prisoner. He had become the Igor of the captain when he got the call. They served as General Colin Powell's personal bodyguards throughout the first gulf war and retired at the same time in 1993. They always said they would get back together and do something big. He dropped everything when he got the call, not that he had anything going on. He had tried the heterosexual life, and it just didn't work for him. He had even gone to his priest for counseling, but that was his undoing. His wife didn't find it very amusing when she walked into the choir room and found them that Friday evening before mass.

Since he messed up the kidnapping of Suzy Fontana and had both of his feet run over, he had not been of much good to the captain. He knew his days were numbered and that it could end in this cold, dark metal relic of the Cold War. The captain didn't tolerate mistakes; he buried them.

Chapter 40

Will Wakes Up with a New Friend

This time Sweet William was loose enough so that he could sit up and move around a bit, but he was still naked. They were in some kind of metal room. It was hard to tell if the room was painted a pale yellow or if it was the soft light of the glow sticks that that hung from the ceiling and lay scattered across the floor. Sweet William waited for the inevitable questions he knew would come. But there were no questions, so Sweet William started with his own questions.

"Can you please tell me what is going on? Why am I here? What did I do? Who are you? Why are you here?" There was a deafening silence. "Why won't you talk to me?"

The other one just looked at him and studied him as he quietly sat on a wooden folding chair. There were three other folding chairs and a folding table against the wall. The whole place smelled musky and stale with a fine dust covering every flat surface. The metal shelves were filled with tightly sealed containers with writing on each of them. Even straining to look, he couldn't read the labels. There were other shelves just like those with dusty cans and bottles.

The glow in the room became softer and softer. Then, finally the other one stood up and shuffled across the room. There was something wrong with his feet. They were big, maybe swollen. It seemed as if every step hurt him. He crossed over to a shelf and picked up another glow stick. He broke the interior glass tube, and as it began to glow, he tossed it at Sweet William's feet. William just looked at him.

Again he asked, "Why won't you talk to me?"

He opened his mouth, and only a groan flowed forth. Sweet William, wide-eyed and stunned, waited until he turned to return to his wooden perch.

Softly he said, "Are you deaf too?," as the big buffoon shuffled away.

There was no answer, no reply, not even a twitch.

"You're a fat pig," Sweet William said a little louder. Then he screamed, "You're a stupid, fat bastard!" Still no response.

Calico Jack sat down, and Sweet William started talking. Just talking about anything that didn't make sense, trying to find out if he really couldn't hear. So he just sat there naked, trying his chains as his roommate went to sleep sitting in the wooden folding chair.

William stood up a little wobbly and pulled at the chain, but it was looped and padlocked around the frame, and the frame was bolted to the floor. He tried to walk around, but he was unsteady, and it just stirred up the dust, so he sat back down. He looked around carefully as his mind cleared and his thoughts became more organized. Then he thought for a while and suddenly recognized some of the bottles. They were old glass ketchup bottles! There were even old Aunt Jemima syrup bottles in the shape of an old Black nanny with a kerchief around her head. He thought and thought and suddenly it came to him like the sermon at the AME Church when he realized he was different from the other boys. He knew exactly where he was.

There was only one underground nuclear fallout shelter on Edisto Island. He was at Prospect Hill Plantation. Mr. Jasper M. Pinckney had installed the fifteen-by-thirty-foot unit during the Cuban Missile Crisis. The only time it was used was the day President Kennedy was shot. He, his wife, and their two girls spent a week in the cramped, little room. It was later cleaned, restocked, and resealed. Mr. Pinckney died before 9-11 or he would have used it again that day.

But now William knew if he could get out, he could get home.

Things were looking up. He looked around again, trying to figure a way out. His companion was nodding off, the situation was getting better still. William quietly tested the lock on the bed. No good, and the chain was welded links. No breaking that. On his leg the chain ended in a regular handcuff. No getting that off. The frame of the bed was bolted together with old square nuts. A bolt was missing on the end closest to the wall, but on the other end he could move both bolts. So he needed a half-inch wrench. With no pockets in his birthday suit, he started to look around. His reach was not much, but he could at least try to find something on the end of the shelf closest to him. There were cans of Spam and Potted Meat as well as peanut butter and jelly, all expired. He thought about when the last time was that he had anything to eat, but strangely he was not hungry. He just wanted to get out. He dug in an old wooden box and found spoons and forks and dinner knives But nothing sharp to use as a weapon and nothing that looked like a wrench. Just as he was getting frustrated and about to give up, he found a "church key" bottle opener, the heavy-metal kind that had a pointed end for making triangular holes in the tops of large juice cans.

William set to work on the end with one bolt, the end furthest away from his roommate. He took the blanket off of the bed and wrapped it around himself as he worked. When he pulled it off, it revealed a gallon of water just under the edge of the bed. He began occasionally taking a drink as he worked on the bolt. It was slow going, and he had been working on it for a while when he started to feel drowsy. He looked at the bottle and noticed the water had a slight pink tinge to it.

"Damn, drugged again," he said as he sat down and leaned against the end of the bed, falling out of consciousness again.

He woke slightly as he felt someone touch him. He also heard a muffled voice speak as he felt large fingers begin to close tightly around his neck.

Chapter 41

Calico Jack's End

When everything was set to interrogate the prisoner inside the plantation house at Prospect Hill, the captain slowly strode out to the old bomb shelter. He was a little concerned about what Calico Jack might try to do but figured he was pretty much beat down after the latest events in his life and would not put up much, or any, of a fight. But to be sure, he quietly unlocked the hatch, then stepped aside and threw the hatch open with a loud clang.

The bright sunshine should have blinded Calico Jack, but he had had a day to think it through. He was ready.

The captain took his heavy Maglite and shone it all around. He listened intently for any sound of Jack or Will moving. There was none. The light flashed around the room high and low and finally settled on Sweet William slumped over the end of the bed. On the far side of the wall was another form lying on the floor and covered in another blanket. He held the light on that form to see if it moved or breathed.

Satisfied that it was too weak to move or was already dead, he switched the flashlight to his left hand and turned to lower himself down the metal ladder. Just as his head was even with the rim of the hatch, there was a motion from the top shelf to the right of the ladder. Then he felt a sharp pain in his left ear.

Jack had waited patiently knowing he had only one chance. He had to catch the captain off guard and then try to get out on his own and to freedom. He swung out with a sack filled with cans. The impact between the captain's shoulders sent his head whipping into the ladder frame and caused him to lose his grip with the one hand. He fell the nine feet and landed on his back, knocking the breath from him. He instantly knew what was happening and could see his attacker pulling himself hand over hand out of the hatch.

He smiled. "You'll have to better than that, Calico Jack," he yelled.

He stood up next to the wall where he had fallen and started for the ladder. Suddenly, he was in the air again. The clothesline that Calico Jack had used to make the trip snare caught him low and only around the right ankle. He was still on the floor, but his leg was up in the air. The counter weight was tied across the metal rafters and consisted of several large twenty-five-pound bags of flour and rice. He reached for his boot knife and quickly freed himself. He quickly started again for the ladder, suddenly stepped on the lard-coated floor, and went right past it, sliding on his ass and into another shelf that came crashing down on top of him. Now, less than amused, he threw the shelf off, carefully slid his feet along the grease-soaked floor, and grabbed the ladder. He quickly started to climb the rungs, feeling the grit underneath his palms. He knew it was some kind of pepper or irritant that he was supposed to rub into his eyes. So, just in case, he closed his eyes until he could feel the sunlight on his face. He bunched himself up at the top and sprang out and onto the sand and grass around the open hatch.

Calico Jack tried to close the hatch, but the captain had wedged it open. He didn't waste any time trying to take the camper that he knew would have a hidden kill switch. He headed for what he felt was his best chance, the old dock and hopefully deep water with a fast outgoing tide. His feet were hurting, but he knew he had to make it or the captain would end it all. Just as his weary feet hit the wooden planks, his legs stopped. He couldn't get them to move, and he began falling. His face hit the old dock, and he could see the blood streaming down the warped boards. He felt cold. Then slowly everything went black.

The second spent .308 case clanged against the hood of the truck. The follow up shot was unneeded but insurance. The captain chambered a third round into the silenced Remington 700 sniper rifle and watched through the scope for any movement, even a twitch. There was none after about five minutes, so he cleared the gun and returned it to its place behind the seat. He casually pushed the gurney down the old path to the dock and lowered it so he could roll the still-warm body on top. He threw the straps across and fastened them securely. No need to have to pick him up again. He made several quick incisions and watched the blood drain into the creek as he contemplated his new problem. He already had one body that was turning up in pieces and causing him enough trouble. This one needed to be put away permanently. As he pushed the lifeless package back to the fallout shelter, he contemplated what to do with it.

Moving Will into the house by himself had taken over an hour, and Jack's misadventure added another half hour to his schedule. He was running out of time. He needed to be back on Edisto for the 7:00 check of the network. He placed the IV into the top of Will's foot and hooked up the liquid lunch with the sedative. Satisfied that all was secure, he locked the doors with his own padlocks. He then unhooked the trailer behind a line of laurels on one of the dirt roads on the property and headed for Edisto Beach.

Late that evening the captain smiled at his own brilliance as he picked the lock at the Parker-Rhoden Funeral Home. Someone should write a book about his exploits. Maybe he would someday. But right now he was thinking about how crazy it was to be breaking into a funeral home. The gurney had some sand on the tires, which he thoughtfully brushed off before he pushed it inside. The room for visitation was already set beautifully, with all three caskets around the room. He pulled out a small digital camera and snapped several pictures. The present teenage inhabitants met their demise in a fiery car crash over the weekend. Their bodies were burned too bad to be viewed, so the caskets were "sealed." It only took ten seconds to pick each lock. He was thankful that they were all in body bags. He uncovered his own three bags, carefully placed one in each of the other caskets, and closed the lids. Locking them back was a little trickier, but he was done in fifteen minutes and sealed each keyhole with drop of superglue for added measure. He put all of the flowers back on the caskets and checked the pictures he had taken to make sure everything was replaced and the room looked just as it had when he arrived. As he locked the outer door behind him, he remembered the old tale of how one Edistonian had gotten all dressed up in his Sunday finest, driven to that same funeral home, and shot himself in the head right in the driveway. The note said he didn't want to be a bother to anyone.

The captain strolled to the far side of the building, and just as he started to get in the camper, he stopped and thought for a moment. He was the only one in the Air Force who knew Calico Jack was gay.

And he knew he was the only one who Jack would have wanted to end his life of lies for him. Reassured that in the end he had done his friend a favor, he headed for Walterboro to plan a little distraction for the nosey sheriff.

Chapter 42

Elevator Music

As he stepped into the elevator, Captain Mikell, dressed as the old camper standing on the outside of the elevator, said, "Don't worry, you can't miss at this range. When the door starts to open, turn the fireman's control key all the way to the left. When it opens, shoot until you run out of bullets as the door closes. Turn the key to the right, and the elevator will take you straight to the garage level. I'll have the van waiting for you to take you to the airport."

"But what if he has a gun?"

"He won't. He'll be coming out of the court room, and no one can take a gun into a court room, not even the sheriff."

"OK. I'll get him this time. He'll pay for killing my Sandy."

"Don't you worry; you'll be set for life in Mexico."

With that, he inserted the override ride key, pressed the button, and stepped back, sending Caleb Donavan to the fourth floor of the Colleton County judicial center.

The captain turned quickly and headed for the faster-service elevator on the other side of the elevator shaft. He entered and inserted his control key. The door closed promptly as he pressed the RT button for the rooftop. When the door opened to the elevator-service room, he grabbed the waiting bag by the access door and climbed into the other side of the elevator shaft. Just as he rehearsed it, the elevator with Caleb was just below him and slowing to stop at the fourth floor. He slid down the cable and softly landed on the roof. He could hear Caleb's excited breathing.

What if he didn't do it? What if he didn't shoot Mallory? It wouldn't matter—he would find another way to derail the investigation. If the detectives found his surveillance boxes on the utility poles, then they would be getting close to finding out about the bomb. If they alerted the Feds, the news would all be over Edisto.

He heard voices outside the elevator. His eyes went cold, and he became almost robotic with his actions.

The elevator door slid open, and there was a gasp.

Caleb yelled, "You killed my Sandy. Now you die!"

The three blank shots that Jeremy fired were not as loud as the two shots the sheriff fired. And those also made the sound of bullets striking the metal elevator as they passed through Caleb. He heard the body hit the floor and the doors close as the elevator moved down. Quickly, he dropped down through the ceiling hatch and grabbed Jeremy. He was hit but not bad enough.

"You said he wouldn't have a gun!"

The captain quickly hit the stop button, grabbed the gun, and tore the nitrite gloves off of Jeremy's hands. As he stuffed the gun and gloves into his left pocket, he drew out a four-inch-long needle from his right boot that he quickly shoved into Caleb's left ear. The needle went straight into his brain, and his entire body went stiff. Just for good measure he shoved it in several more times at different angles before putting it back into his boot.

He hit the stop button again to restart the elevator, grabbed the edge of the ceiling hatch, and pulled himself up quickly and replaced the cover. This time, just in case someone got curious, he stuck a small bolt in the latch. The elevator moved to the garage, and when the door opened there were shouts from the security officers: "Freeze! Put your hands up! Step out where we can see you."

Then silence.

Someone spoke softly. "He's on the floor and not moving."

Another said, "I don't see the gun."

"He's hit; lot of blood on the floor."

"OK, but move in slowly."

Just as the first officer reached in and touched the lifeless body, the other elevator came down and the door opened. Mallory was holding the door back with one hand and had his service pistol in the other.

"It's OK, Sheriff. He's dead."

The captain suddenly relaxed and stepped to the other elevator roof. The door closed, and it started to move up.

The next day there was an inquiry held, and the sheriff was put on an indefinite leave of absence. The solicitor's office was not sure how to proceed, but they knew they needed time and to also keep the sheriff out of sight of the news cameras until they could figure it out.

Why did the sheriff shoot an unarmed man in an elevator? There were no other eye witnesses to the event. None of the people who heard the shots were sure how many there had been or who fired them. There were no bullet holes behind where the sheriff had been standing. There was no gun powder residue on the victim's hands.

Sheriff Mallory, at home, sat in his favorite recliner, staring into his iced tea, and asked, "What the hell is going on?"

Chapter 43

Will in the Hospital

Sweet William did wake up again, this time with white sheets and in a clean little room. It could have been a hospital room since he was in what seemed to be a hospital bed. He tried to move but was again restricted by the bed's restraints. He could scratch his nose and bend his knees a little, but he couldn't get off the bed. There was strap across his waist that pinned him firmly to the bed.

He was a little thirsty but not hungry at all. He had no idea how much time had passed since he was first taken and why he wouldn't be hungry. Then he realized that there was an IV in the top of his foot. The bag was at the end of the bed. He didn't try to figure anything out; he just looked around. Realizing that there was probably some sort of drug in the IV, he just relaxed and let it happen. He was warm, and there were no pigs around.

Once again his spirits lifted, and he felt that things were getting better. He began to think maybe he had been rescued.

The door opened and what looked like a doctor with a surgical mask walked in and went straight to the IV. He adjusted the flow valve and took William's pulse from his ankle. Satisfied with that, he pulled on something that tightened all the restraints holding Will at once. He then took out a huge syringe with a yellow substance in it. It didn't have a lot of medicine in it. And Will felt only the pressure, not the pain of the needle penetrating his vein at the top of his other foot. He watched the yellow substance slowly drain into his body. When it was all gone, the "doctor" didn't pull it out. He slowly started to draw out Will's blood. He carefully let the syringe fill to the top, then removed it and placed a small, circular Band-Aid on the puncture. He left the room without a word. Will passed out again.

When he awoke this time, he was still in the same bed with most of the restraints loosened again. There was no IV in his foot anymore, just the needle and the connection port. There was just a small stain of blood on the sheet. The door opened again, and another figure came in. This one was dressed as an artist with a dark-green smock-type coat over old jeans. He wore a red beret and a colorful scarf around his neck and face. The dark glasses masked his eyes, so there was no knowing his intent. He said nothing; he just pulled out some brushes and a small steel bowl and began to work. He acted like he was painting, but there was no paint.

Then he stopped, looked at Will, and pulled out a big syringe with a dark-red substance in it. It took a while, but suddenly, and with a shutter, he realized it was his blood. The artist squirted some of it into his small bowl, rolled it around, and started to paint. At first Will couldn't understand what the images were after seeing the blood. Then he saw that it was a cartoon-type drawing of a falling bomb. Then, he recognized the radioactive symbol that appeared on the bomb. The artist began to write over the image, in letters a foot tall, the name "Davies." None of it made any since to him. Radioactive bomb and someone named Davies? Davies, atom bomb, he was lost. Then, as the artist wrote "Kevin" in front of Davies, Will panicked and began to shake violently. It all started to come back to him in floods of emotions and torrents of pain. The hate, the love…the fear! "NOOOO!" he screamed.

Chapter 44

Kevin

Kevin Davies was an old flame in more ways than one. William met him at Patrick's, the gay bar in Charleston. They immediately became lovers, and William felt on top of the world. The relationship continued, and they did everything together. Well, almost. Kevin loved to scuba dive, but William was claustrophobic and panicked every time he went underwater. Kevin was understanding and didn't pressure him into diving. They would go out diving from Kevin's boat, and William would sit patiently, looking out over the water and waiting for his friend. He was always excited to see Kevin come up. For one, he would be relieved that Kevin was OK, and more than that, he looked good in his black-and-gray skintight wet suit. They always seemed to end up at St. Helena Sound near Otter Island.

Each time they went, Kevin had some new contraption to use to explore the depths. One day Kevin asked William to meet him at Steamboat Landing. When Will arrived, there was a shrimp boat there, just off the end of the boat ramp. Kevin was on the bow waving anxiously for Will to swim out. Will immediately jumped in and swam to the boat. Kevin helped him aboard and told him about a surprise he had for Will.

"Where did you get this shrimp boat?"

"I borrowed it from Mr. Chang on Shem Creek. I have to have it back tomorrow night."

They started off on the shrimp boat and went out past Deveaux Bank and into the open water heading south. William was full of questions, but Kevin kept brushing them off and smiling. Once they reached the end of Edisto Beach, Kevin swung the boat into St Helena Sound and plowed up the river into the outgoing tide that was about to turn. Quickly, Kevin looked around as if searching for markers and finally pointed and shouted, "There it is." He steered for the old milk jug and released the anchor. The boat swung around and tightened down on the anchor line. Kevin was in the water before Will could ask what was going on. He only had to wait a short time. As quick as he went in, Kevin came out but this time with a look Will had never seen. He was all business and started to bark orders at William. A little put off by it, William did as he was directed and lowered the center net straight down from the boom. Kevin was back in the water again before Will had time to think about what was going on. The net was waving all through the water, and Kevin could be seen near the surface moving it around. Suddenly, Kevin broke to the surface and told Will to hit the lever to raise the net: "Count to ten, then pull it back to stop and set the lock." Will did exactly what he was told and then stepped aside and looked out over the rows of houses far in the distance on the beach. He stood there with his arms folded, sniffling as if his feelings had been put through a laundry wringer. Kevin jumped in the boat, ran up to the controls, and raised his prize a little higher but not totally out of the water. He ran to the wheel house, engaged the prop, and moved slowly up Fish Creek. Around the turn the boat slowed to a crawl and stopped. Kevin, still in his diving gear, went back in the water and was gone for another brief time. All the while Will was getting more angry that he didn't know what was going on and was being ignored. This time when Kevin came up, he dumped the scuba gear and ran to the controls. He hit the freefall on the boom, and the weight of whatever was in the net spun the reel like a top. As soon as the cable went slack, Kevin ran to the back, climbed up on the boom, and released the net. The back of the boat sprang up from the released weight. Kevin ran to the wheel house again and started backing the shrimp boat out of the little inlet. Kevin was all smiles, and Will was all frowns.

Back out of the sound, Kevin tied off the wheel and went to Will.

"I'm sorry; I just had to get this thing done."

"What thing? What's so important that you had to be rude to me?"

"Well, let's just say I have secured my retirement."

"What, did you find a treasure chest?"

"Sort of, but this one glows in the dark." Puzzled, William turned to look away to signal his disgust with Kevin. "I'm sorry, William, in more ways than you can imagine. You have been a great help in me finding my treasure. And you didn't even know it. All those times you were talking about your father, Air Force Colonel Howard Richardson, you didn't think I was listening, but I was. I listened to every word, especially about how he almost crashed the big jet here at Edisto, how he had to drop such an important piece of equipment just to stay airborne and save the rest of the crew."

Chapter 45

The Bomb (Historically True*)

It was 1958, and the B-47 bomber was on a simulated combat mission from Homestead Air Reserve Base in Florida. It was carrying a single 7,600-pound thermonuclear bomb. At about 2:00 a.m., the B-47 collided with its escort, an F-86 fighter jet. The F-86 crashed after the pilot ejected from the plane, but the B-47, despite being heavily damaged, remained airborne but only barely. The crew requested permission to jettison the bomb in order to reduce weight and prevent the bomb from exploding during the emergency landing. Permission was granted, and the bomb was jettisoned at 7,200 feet while the bomber was traveling about two hundred knots. The crew reported that they did not see an explosion when the bomb struck the sea. They managed to land the battered B-47 safely at Hunter Army Airfield in Savannah. The pilot, Colonel Howard Richardson, was awarded the Distinguished Flying Cross after this incident for his role in piloting the B-47 and saving the crew.

Two days later, over one hundred Navy personnel equipped with handheld sonar and galvanic radioactive sensors began an intensive search for the huge bomb. Two months later the military announced that the search efforts had been unsuccessful. The Air Force determined that it was better to leave the bomb covered in mud at the bottom of the sea floor than to disturb it and risk potential detonation or contamination. It contained four hundred pounds of conventional high explosives and highly enriched uranium. It also contained a plutonium trigger.

Chapter 46

The Thanks William Gets

"You made all of this possible. I could have never done it without you. And now I have to repay you for all that you have done." William still wouldn't turn around; he was in full pout mode.

Kevin pulled a small pistol out of the wheel house, raised it to the center of Will's back, and thought, *Maybe it's better this way.* As he squeezed the trigger, the boat struck the sandbar, and the shot was off. Miraculously the bullet went wide and only lightly grazed Wills left side. But the force of the boat grounding knocked all of the booms and winches off their resting mounts, and the heavy tools flew out of the old wooden box on top of the wheel house. They came down like rain with the first sledge hammer hitting Kevin's shooting arm just above the wrist, breaking both bones cleanly. The gun, of course, went flying to parts unknown. The big sixteen-inch pipe wrench came down on William's head with a wicked crack. The wooden beams that held the winch in place had broken, and the old oak boards had splintered into so many needlelike spikes. Kevin looked at his broken arm and at William still on his feet but stumbling toward the port gunnel. He knew William was dead from such a blow to the head. But to make sure, he wanted to see his blood. He couldn't afford for him to live. Looking around, he found the big butcher knife that was stuck in the crack by the wheel house. As he reached for it, the boat shifted and he lost his balance. He was heading headfirst into the splintered oak. He struggled to catch his footing, but there was nothing to stop him. He flailed with his arms trying to fly backward. But there was no reversing his momentum.

Will came back to conscious just soon enough to see his lover's head being impaled on the bed of splinters. There was one splinter where his left eye had been and another that came out of his mouth. Will was confused, distraught, and not feeling so well.

The boat shifted as it passed over the sandbar, and Will was being thrown again toward the side of the boat, but he caught his balance, and just as he righted himself, he turned and a big Igloo cooler slammed into his chest and took him off the boat. The water woke him completely, and he realized the precariousness of situation. The cooler was next to him, and he grabbed it and hung on as the incoming tide pushed him toward Bay Creek. He just held on and tried not to think of anything that just happened. As he floated further upstream, he guided the cooler toward the beach by kicking his feet. As he got closer he could see there was no one on the beach. Just as well, he thought. He didn't want to have to explain anything to anyone. The cooler came to rest in the surf, and Will just crawled up out of the water and rolled over so the sun could shine on his face. He had no idea how long he lay there, but eventually he sat up and looked at the small wound on his side. The cooler was still in the surf just below him. He knew it had something in it by the way it sat in the water. He staggered over and popped the latch. Inside were the chopped up remains and head of the shrimp boat owner, Mr. Chang.

William knew he didn't want any part of that, so he closed the lid and pushed it out. Then he made his way up to the Bay Point Villas. He stood in the elevator with the door closed for a while and then hit a random button. The whirl of the cables was reassuring. When the bell rang he stepped out, turned to the left, and started down the hall. He tried one door, and it was locked. He tried another, and it swung open. He stepped in and closed the door behind him. This condo had been vacant for a while. It was musky and the air was stale. There were cards from every real estate company on Edisto laid out across the counter. It was one of the condos that they just couldn't sell. He walked into the bathroom and looked at himself. He was quite a mess. His lip was cut but not too bad. His head hurt and there was a rising bump; it was very tender. His T-shirt was bloody where he had been shot. He mustered the nerve and took a look; it was more like a big scratch. He searched underneath the bathroom counter and found some peroxide that he dabbed on the wound. In the kitchen he found a first-aid kit with a large bandage that he used to cover it. He started to plunder through the drawers in the other room. He found some clean but musky-smelling summer clothes that were a little too small for him. He put them on, lay down on the bed, and started to cry like a girl.

Chapter 47

Will Tells All

Now strapped down in what seemed like a hospital, he knew what this was all about. That damned old bomb. But what could he do? He had no idea what was coming next.

But it came quick. The question mark on the wall let him know that he had better start telling the whole story.

"OK, OK, I got it! Kevin must have found the bomb. He stole a shrimp boat and somehow put the bomb in the trawlers net and took it up Fish Creek to hide it. But that was years ago. It could be lost again, or the corrosion could have eaten it away. I don't know."

He started to cry again. The artist left, and in a flash the doctor came back in. This time he hooked an IV to William's foot and left the open end hanging over a mason jar. The blood dripped slowly. Will was getting scared he would bleed to death. The doctor laughed and left the room. Will's gaze was fixed on the jar. He started to feel cold as his blood began to fill the jar. Then, quietly, the old camper guy came in and just looked at the jar. He turned, looked at Will, and said, "Tell me more!"

Chapter 48

Warren Thinks

So, Warren thought, *could it be? Why would anyone want a nuclear bomb? Well, a terrorist for one. Dictators for two. And what could it be worth? Millions? Billions? That has to be it!* But now what was he going to do with his newfound knowledge? Warren still hadn't mentioned the lost atom bomb to Detective McKee.

Chapter 49

The Detective and the Boxes

Bo had gone home but was still mending his wounds. Warren wasn't sure if he should even approach him about what he figured out. So he did what he would always do when he knew he shouldn't—he did it anyway.

The lawman listened with a wry dismissive smile at first, but after he opened the grocery bag and saw the box with the electronics and camera, his smile faded. The first thing he did was limp over to his computer and get on the internet. He searched the words on the camera and got hits right away. They were expensive, and the batteries were even more expensive. The Geiger counter was only a couple hundred compared to the thousands the other components would have cost.

"Altogether this package is close to two grand," he told Warren. "How many of these things have you found?"

"Last count was six; four look just like this one, and two are a little different."

"How so?"

"Smaller but longer."

"Where are those?"

"On Point Street by the beach accesses."

"Hmm, maybe we should install our own cameras," said the detective thoughtfully.

"You got that kinda money?"

"No, but I do have some game cameras we use to scout for deer. They work day or night and twenty-four hours a day."

"How you gonna set them up?" asked Warren

"I'm not; you are. Go get them out of the shed out back. Here's the key."

And with that, Warren went out the back door to look for a box labeled "hunting stuff." It took a while to find it because he was so impressed by all of the other boxes so neatly stacked with the name "Freedia" on them. Although very tidy and organized, he could tell some had been opened and resealed a lot. Those were the ones closest to the door. The top of one was taped, but he could see lace were the top flaps didn't quite meet. It was dirty with what looked like the green pluff mud on Pine Island.

He came back with the "hunting stuff" box filled with game cameras and never mentioned the other ones. Bo was too wrapped up in checking the game cameras to see Warren's troubled look. He pulled out each of the four cameras and checked the batteries and the memory cards. To be sure that they worked, he pointed each one of them at Warren and waited the fifteen-second-delay time to hear the shutter cycle. Once satisfied they all worked, he locked the lids down and put them back in the box.

"Here. Go put these were they can take a picture of anyone looking at or climbing the poles. It's a long shot, but maybe our mystery man will come to check on them. Hey! Clip some wires on the one you took, and hang it back were you got it from. And put two of these game cameras on that one."

"Well, I have to get the cherry picker back to do that."

"Hmm, yeah, better yet, don't put it back! He'll spend more time looking on the ground for it. Now put these up when there are a lot of people around. You know, act like nothing's happening, and just strap them to a tree or pole out of sight."

"OK, I'm not going to get in trouble doing this, am I?"

"Nah. If anyone asks, just tell them you are trying to get a picture of the albino deer that was seen on Point Street."

"Ok I'll do it tomorrow."

"Good now maybe we can get some idea of who's doing this."

"I'm starting to feel better anyway so I'll be driving around keeping an eye on the other ones. Now where are those other boxes?"

Warren explained as best he could remember the location of each of the devices. Bo thanked him for helping and abruptly sent him on his way.

Warren never liked feeling dismissed, not even in school or the army. So he went to Whaley's to think about it and look for answers in the bottom of a glass. After the second beer he decided to go home via the pole he had taken the box from. Just for fun he took one of the game cameras and hung it on a fencepost under the laurels that grew there. Realizing how easy it was, he put another one across the parking lot, looking back at the pole.

Satisfied, he started to drive home. Then he said, "Oh, what the hell?" and went around and placed the others. He and Pugzie stopped by the Piggly Wiggly and got a box of Mrs. Mack's fried chicken. They ate most of it on the way home.

Chapter 50

Detective Bo Goes Out

Bo McKee left home the next day for his first venture since the accident. He first stopped by JJ's Garage, and while he was waiting on his leaking tire to get plugged, he noticed a bunch of guys standing around an old Ford Pinto laughing their butts off. He walked over to see what was so funny. He couldn't figure out why everyone was laughing at JJ pouring gas into the car.

JJ turned, acted startled by his presence, and quickly put the gas can behind his back.

"JJ, what are you doing to Thomas's Pinto?" asked Bo.

"Oh, just a little brotherly love, officer. I just put two more gallons of gas in his tank for him."

At that everyone started laughing even louder. Confused, Bo just looked at JJ for an answer. And he had a doozy.

"You know, my brother has been working on this old Pinto for a long time. Well, right after he got it running again, he was bragging about how good his gas mileage was. He'd come in almost every week and say 'I got twenty-eight miles to the gallon on this tank.' Every few days we got another report, even if we didn't want to hear about it. So we decided to play a little joke on him."

"What kinda joke?" he asked.

"A harmless trick of siphoning off a little bit of gas from his car every time he filled up. But the funny part was we kept taking out a little more each week. He got down to twelve miles to the gallon. Then he went and rebuilt the carburetor again. So we did the honorable thing and we returned the gas we had taken, a little bit at a time. Each time we just added a little more. He's getting an amazing sixty-two miles to the gallon now. He said he called *Popular Mechanics*, and they want to see his car and check the mileage themselves."

They all laughed until they cried. Bo just shook his head in disbelief and went back to his car. He gave JJ's wife a twenty on a fifteen-dollar bill for the tire repair. She thanked him and just looked at her husband, then back at the detective. They both smiled, and he left.

Chapter 51

Bo and Warren Look at the Cameras

He drove down to Bay Point and looked for the game cameras. He didn't see them, so he drove to Warren's house. Warren's old truck wasn't there, and he didn't feel like getting out, so he drove back to the beach and parked looking out over the ocean by the Pavilion. He thought about a lot of things: the murder, the missing gay waiter, the pig in the road, and, of course, his Freedia. He thought about her a lot this time of year; it was close to the time of year when she died.

After two days he found Warren and told him in no uncertain terms to get all of the cameras and bring them to his house so they could look at the results. Warren arrived at his house just before dark.

They loaded the pictures from the game cameras onto his computer and then started to look at them carefully. The cameras showed nothing suspicious, but they did have lots of pictures, over two hundred of them.

But, as usual, Warren noticed something suspicious right away. There were several different people wearing the same hat.

Once it was an old man patting his pockets as if he had lost something, another was a middle-aged man with a cooler, looking around calling for somebody, and another was a young man with a metal detector. But how often do you see a USC cap with the brim and edges all torn up to make it look old and worn? Nah, not the black and garnet of the University of South Carolina but garnet and gold. The colors of the University of Southern California!

When Warren pointed it out to the detective, he almost ran with his one good leg to the desk for his notebook. He quickly flipped the pages to where his investigation had begun. And there it was—Sonny Cartwright said the mystery guy they and the others had dinner with had a University of Southern California ring.

This could be the big break he was looking for. But he couldn't arrest someone for going to the wrong school. He needed more evidence, and right now that was in short supply. So they set out the cameras again.

This time the old camper man showed up on several of them wearing the old USC hat. Now he had a stronger connection, but it was still not enough.

How could he find out more? He needed a plant, a mole, someone who could get close to this guy and get some details. But who was he anyway? Was he old, middle-aged, or young? The old camper guy never talked to anyone and had been coming around for the past few years. He had to find a way to find out more.

"Warren, you have to make contact with this guy."

"What?" he asked in a surprised tone.

"You have to do what you do best. Talk to this stranger and get to know him. Get some background on where he came from, what he's doing here, that sort of stuff."

Warren looked puzzled at first, then very matter-of-factly answered, "I'm not a cop or a deputy. I'm just trying to figure out what's going on. You need to do it yourself or get one of the undercover cops ya'll have."

Bo, remembering that the sheriff had said no backup or anything, thought for a minute.

"Well, the sheriff's already said I get no help. I can't get anybody without him ordering it, and he's still on leave after shooting the guy in the elevator. So we have to do it. We have to find out what happened to Cecil and who blew up Mr. Beal."

"Not we. Not me. You have to do it or get it done." With that Warren stood up to leave. "I was just doing this for fun."

The lawman responded with authority: "It's your civic duty to help an officer in need."

Warren laughed at the attempt and stepped out the door. "Nope."

Chapter 52

Warren Goes for Coffee

The detective knew he needed to tie the old camper guy in with the cameras and radiation detectors. If he could, then he might be able to bring him in and question him legitimately. He wasn't sure of the exact statute in the law, but he was sure that if you can't put up a yard sale flyer on a utility pole, then you can't put up some expensive surveillance box. He might even be able to use some federal terrorist law like the Patriot Act.

Outside Warren sat in his truck and thought about what Bo had said, not that he should be a good citizen but that they needed more information. Pugzie had been waiting in the truck and looked like he needed a beer. So they drove down to Coots and parked on the southern side of the Pavilion this time.

The old Datsun camper was sitting there. Warren looked at it and tried to see something that wasn't there: a big clue. So, not seeing anything, he and Pugzie took the stairs and went into Coots. There, at the closest end of the bar, sat the old camper dude with a cup of coffee. He had never seen him in there before. Warren instinctively headed for his usual spot, right in front of the beer taps.

Margaret, the bartender, was already pouring Pugzie's beer into his special bowl. As she handed it to Warren, he thanked her and asked a question that no one had ever heard him ask.

"Miss Margaret, could I have a cup of coffee instead of a beer, please?"

She looked surprised at first, then smiled and hustled off to make it from the one-cup fancy brewer that was just installed.

"Smelled so good I just had to try that newfangled contraption," he said loud enough for the old camper to hear. He looked down the bar to see if there was a response.

Captain Mikell looked over and raised his cup in a salute to reply.

When Margaret returned with the steaming cup, she asked, "Cream? Sugar?"

Warren, taking advantage of the comment, said, "You callin' me sugar? I like that."

In fact, Warren had always had an eye for the tall, slim redhead. She was much younger than him, and he knew it was just a fantasy. But who wouldn't be captivated by her? She was smart, funny, and very pleasant. He had seen her at the Easter Sunrise Service all dressed in white, and he was sure it was an angel. Anyway, it was his fantasy and he liked it.

The young couple at the other end of the bar got up to go out on the pier. As they opened the door, the salt air flowed through the room, mixed with the aroma of the coffee, and made it taste even better.

"So how ya been?" he asked the angel of his dreams.

"Same as yesterday and the day before. Business is slowing down, and the local excitement has died down too."

"Yeah, you heard anymore?" he asked watching closely as she bent over the sink in front of him.

She looked up from rinsing glasses. "No, nothing on Mr. Beal. Everyone is still in shock that he was a drug dealer. Melvin, the chef, said the drugs might have been planted, but Ira said what was in there was worth $20,000, and no one would have let that much get away. They could have fingered him with much less than that. There's talk of having a memorial service here on the beach next week for Cecil. But I think they're waiting to see if anything else washes up or if Sweet William turns up."

Warren looked in the mirror behind the bar to see if there was a reaction from the other end of the bar. Nothing.

He pushed the conversation further: "I hear the U.S. Department of Energy may be coming here with a bunch of people toward the end of the month."

"For what?" she asked, shaking the water from a glass and giving Warren a show.

"To look for the Tybee bomb again," he lied. "They have to come back every so often to try to locate it."

Now there was a reaction from the other end of the bar. The back grew straight and the eyes grew cold. He pushed a little harder.

"Heard someone say over at Dockside that some strange pieces of metal with numbers on them were found over on Pine Island. They weren't sure if they were part of the bomb or the old World War II fighter that crashed years ago."

"Well, we could sure use the business," Margaret offered.

The old camper stood up, pulled out a few bills, and said "Keep the change, Miss" in a voice much younger than his looks.

As soon as the old camper went out the door, Warren asked "Can you watch Pugzie? I gotta go to the men's," and he hurried to the door. He looked out first to make sure the coast was clear, then went out. Instead of going right to the restrooms, he went straight to the deck alongside the bar, where it was dark and he could see the parking lot. The old camper guy was slowly walking past Warren's truck and looking at it carefully. He stopped, looked closely in Warren's passenger window, then walked on and opened up the back of the camper and went in.

Warren went back into the bar and made an excuse that the coffee had upset his constitution and he and Pugzie would have to leave.

"Don't worry about the tab," Margaret offered. "I'm glad you came in."

Warren picked up Pugzie and almost ran to his truck. He wanted to stay and talk to Margaret, but he knew he had to get his truck away to keep it from getting an explosive gift package or something else. As soon as he opened the door and put the old bulldog in, the camper door swung open, and the old camper guy stepped out with a box.

Warren put on his best face and smiled big to his new acquaintance. The smile was not offered back. He quickly backed out of the parking lot and didn't look back until he was around the corner on the causeway heading out of town. It didn't look like he was being followed, but to be sure he pulled into the Edistonian behind the diesel pumps, where it was darkest. Twenty minutes went by, and only the mayor and his secretary's cars came by headed back to the beach about ten minutes apart. *Well,* he thought, *after twenty years, they're still at it.*

Satisfied that there was no threat, he drove home carefully, just in case the truck had been tampered with. When he pulled into the long driveway, he looked for any other tire tracks. Not seeing any, he drove right up to the door. Pugzie jumped out and was scratching at the screen door as he came up the steps. He opened the door, and there was a loud bang. Warren dove inside. He crawled across the floor to the kitchen to get his baseball bat. Then he saw the mop handle lying across the floor. That's all it was—the mop had fallen over, and the noise was the handle hitting flat on the floor. He stood up and kicked the mop for scaring him.

Chapter 53

How Cecil Went, and Mikell Goes Fishing

Cecil had found an access hatch to the plutonium trigger capsule of the bomb with the serial number 47782, which matched the serial number on all of the related documents as well as on Wikipedia. Cecil, always looking for a way to make a buck, let certain people in Savannah, Georgia, know he had something for sale. The old camper guy showed up with a handful of cash and tried to buy it from Cecil. Thinking he could hold out for more, Cecil gave the metal plate to Suzy Fontana for safe keeping as he tried to drive up the price. He didn't realize that once the old camper guy had seen that the serial number matched the bomb, the part lost its value and where it had been found became very valuable.

The old camper guy (Captain Mikell) and Calico Jack tortured Cecil on an old dock barge to find out where he had found the bomb part.

Once he told them where he found the part and all he knew, the captain started to take the pressure off the four large anchors and weights that held his arms and legs. But the old frayed cable became hung up on the port boom's pulley. Calico Jack climbed the boom to free the stuck cable. He hit it, shook it, and it released…quickly…and in the wrong way. Cecil came apart…literally.

The next morning, after having coffee with Warren the previous night, the captain went down to the docks just after sunrise. He was hanging out at Waterfront Sports and Dockside trying to find if anyone knew what was on Otter Island and how to get there. He realized he had arrived too early, after finding no one there. He knew all of the locals would be at the Sea Cow if they weren't at the docks. He had never been in the place, so he changed his disguise. This time he changed into one he had never used—himself: kaki button-down shirt, Levi's, and crocks with socks.

Wednesdays were liars breakfast day. The locals always came in to find ways to screw up the tourist business. They hated anyone who came to the beach, everyone except, of course, their friends and families.

Captain Mikell ordered the big breakfast, picked up the local paper, and started to listen. Most of the talk was about keeping money from the town's advertising account. There was also hushed talk about raiding the Chamber of Commerce funds and the town's sewer account. As he realized none of this was doing him any good, the locals began to leave and his breakfast arrived. He knew he had to eat some of it to not seem suspicious.

As he thought of how to get to his treasure, he ate the breakfast and decided he needed more time to think, so he ordered the biscuits and gravy. His ideas were becoming clearer now. An order of buckwheat pancakes, and he had it.

When he woke up about three in the afternoon, after such a big breakfast, he realized he had been had. He almost lost another day of trying to get to the bomb. He quickly got up, checked his look, and went back to the docks. By 4:00 he heard enough to make a plan. Apparently, his coffee friend was heading for Otter Island and "the spot." Captain Bob Sanders was going to take him to the exact spot he had missed, and this time put him right on it. He had heard it all while sitting on the john at the Thirsty Fish. They didn't know he was in there when they made their secret plan.

What Bob was doing was taking Warren to his mother's house to show him the spot of peeling paint he had been unable to locate when he went there the first time. It was a small place, but she wanted it repaired.

The captain went down to Watersports and asked about renting a boat again. But this time Maggy wasn't letting him get away. He looked different, but she was sure it was the same guy.

"Sorry, there's only the Mako left, and that boat is a charter boat and only goes out with a captain. The smaller rental boat is out on the water."

"I need to charter that one now. Is there a captain around?" he asked.

"Only me, and I'm available. Where do you want to go, and what do you want to do?"

He thought for a second, then said, "Where Captain Bob goes. Around Fish Creek on Otter Island, I believe. I hear the flounder fishing is good."

She thought for a second about trying to see if he would insist on Otter, so she offered, "There are better spots I know and closer too. The weather is not looking too good later on, and we might get caught in it."

"No, Otter will be fine. That's where I want to go," he insisted.

"OK, it's your dime. Fill out this form, and I need your driver's license." He handed her the license, took the clipboard with the form, and began to fill it out.

She bent down behind the counter and opened the cover to the all-in-one printer. She hit the scan/print button on the printer and also started the email program. She rose up, handed him his license, bent down again, and quickly punched in Detective McKee's email address. She hit the send button and got the copy and stapled it to the form he handed back.

"You need bait and tackle?" she asked.

"Sure," he replied, "whatever we need to catch the big ones."

She grabbed a rod and reached for the frozen cigar minnows. "Beer?"

"No, just water," he yelled back as he headed for his silver Land Rover. He returned with a long bag and a backpack.

She came on board with the fishing gear and cranked the engine. As soon as he was seated and she had checked everything, she jumped back on the dock and cast off the lines.

I should take the boat now, he thought, then realized it could cause a big commotion and sound an alarm. So he let her back out the boat and headed for the island. As they slowed to pass the sandbar in front of Otter Island, he checked his bags to be sure the shotgun was loaded and ready.

The skies were darkening quickly from the south as they arrived. "Might not get much fishing in," she offered.

"Well, let's make the most of it," he replied and pulled out his Geiger counter. He moved it around and started giving her directions when they arrived at Fish Creek. He motioned for her to continue up Fish Creek.

Strange GPS, she thought. She eased up the creek, following his directions, and dropped the anchor when he told her to.

The boat swung around as the line tightened with the outgoing tide. He pulled out another strange device. She was sure now that this was no fishing trip and that it could be getting dangerous. She backed away from the controls and sat on the gunnel closest to the deepest part of the channel.

He was too busy with his devices to see that she was getting into a position to jump overboard if she needed to. She lowered another anchor without him seeing. If she had to swim, she wanted to slow the boat as much as she could. She acted as if she were checking the fuel tank and unplugged it but left it hanging so it looked normal.

Suddenly, he looked around and saw her just standing there. His face went blank, and he tore the VHS radio off of the console. She hit the water at the same time the radio did. A few strokes and she dove as deep as she could. She didn't hear any gun shots, but she knew she was in trouble. She broke the surface only when she had to and saw him struggling with the anchor lines. She started swimming with the tide and was putting a lot of distance between them. She didn't look back but heard the motors fire up. They roared to life, and she could tell the boat was turning toward her. At the first sound of the motor running out of gas, she dove again. No motor sounds, no gunshots, maybe she was far enough away to be somewhat safe. When she broke to the surface again, the first lightning and thunderclap sounded the sky was dark. She swam toward Pine Island where the water was too shallow for the boat and where there were trees and brush right up to the water's edge.

The powerless boat was beginning to drift away from her. He looked quickly in the growing darkness and saw the unconnected fuel line. As soon as he plugged it back in and gave the bulb a squeeze, the motor fired right up again.

Chapter 54

The Search for Maggy

Captain Jamie Springer had been looking for Maggy and the Mako off Pine Island when he saw the phosphorous light from the boats jinxing and going crazy around Otter Island. Bo McKee had called him and told him something was up. He knew it was either a bunch of drunks caught in the storm, or Maggy in trouble. He was always pulling people off the sandbar and thought, *Why should this night should be any different?* He grabbed the box that held the FLIR thermal-vision headset. It was all he got from the town when they asked him to become the rescue boat for the surrounding waters. He placed it on his head, hit the power button, and in two seconds could see everything that had a temperature higher than the surrounding water's 78 degrees. The boats and people where clearly visible, but in a negative black and white view. His seventeen-foot Boston Whaler was over powered by the 115 horsepower, 4 stroke Yamaha motor, and it leapt onto plane like a race horse. He was on the scene in less than two minutes. Quickly, he saw the Mako heading for a man overboard. But the speed was too high to be a rescue. Recognizing that the boat was going to try to run over the person in the water, he slammed the throttle to full and headed for the swimmer. His detailed thermal unit also allowed him to see a big center console on an intercept course from the north, at about 11:00 from his angle, heading for the sandbar.

Bekka had been waiting for the smugglers pick-up boat she knew was coming from her friends at Hilton Head. She spotted the plastic-wrapped bales that had been hidden in the low brush. She knew by the waves breaking over the bar that it was about a foot underwater. The sandbar had shifted over the years, but it was always deep on both sides. She knew the timing because she had jumped it so many times before. It was one of her favorite ways to release her anger and was perfect for the jump. She throttled back to wait in the dark.

Springer came around the bend without lights and just hundred yards behind the Mako as it turned for another attempt to hit the swimmer. The other boat was moving in their direction fast. He punched the release on the two permanently mounted parachute flares to distract the other boats. It worked. Both boats seemed to throttle back surprised, not expecting the bright flashes seconds apart. His goggles saved him from the flash. Stunning them with the bright flares gave him just enough time to throw out a ring and hope that the swimmer could catch on. He trimmed the engine back and turned to let the line drift into the swimmer. As soon as he felt the added weight on the line, he backed down and yelled, "Get in the ring and hang on."

Chapter 55

Maggy Gets Picked Up

Maggy was underwater when the flares went off, when she broke the surface she saw a bright-yellow rope in the water coming by in front of her on top of the waves, reflected in the bright light. She grabbed for the line frantically and felt it burn through her fingers until the first of the three knots came to her. She felt the line straighten as she grabbed it tight after the third knot. It began to drag her underwater, but she held on. Just knowing it was a ski line by her years of living on the water made her grip it like it was the last thing on Earth. It towed her only briefly, then it stopped. She was confused until she heard the voice yelling. Maggy knew it was Springer, and she also knew she was saved. She quickly put both arms through the ring and grabbed the line. The line went tight again. She pulled herself up on the ring and started to skim across the waves like she did on so many a Sunday afternoons. The ride was brief, and the line went slack again. Suddenly, she felt a strong arm around her waist pushing her up a ladder. She spilled onto the floor and started coughing and screaming.

"He's trying to kill me! He's gonna kill me!"

"Who?" yelled Springer.

"The guy who rented the boat is trying to kill me!" She started trying to explain what happened.

Springer was half listening as he grabbed his thermal headset and jammed it on his head again. He turned quickly to get his bearings with the lights of the Bay Creek Villas and the line of beach houses. He pulled Maggy to her feet and stuffed her between himself and the console as he cranked the wheel hard to starboard and headed for safety. He held her tight, looked back to see two boats coming together at high speed, and wondered who the hell was in the other boat.

Chapter 56

Bekka Meets Capt. Mikell

The captain looked down from the burning flares but couldn't see anything except blinding dots from looking into the bright lights. He knew better than to look up at a flare; he cursed his stupidity. His military training taught him to shield his eyes from flares. He blinked and rubbed his eyes, trying to find his target. But only the area right around him was lit, everything beyond thirty yards was blinded by the rain reflecting the light of the flares. The thunder continued to roar overhead.

Bekka launched the Contender off the sandbar that ran out from Otter Island at over forty knots toward the stern of the other boat. It flew like an Osprey that had spotted a floundering fish. Straight and true it came at the smaller Mako from above and slightly across his port side. It hit three feet from where he was standing behind the center console. There was an awful crunching sound when it landed. The impact broke the boat completely in half and sent the front of the boat rocketing skyward and back toward the bank of Otter Island. But just as it reached the peak of its flight, the anchor line that was tangled with the motors went taught briefly, then snapped. The bow of the broken boat started to spin like a top. The captain held on to the console and tried to figure out what hit him when he lost his grip. Disoriented and having been thrown out into the darkness, he instinctively pulled himself into a ball and waited for the impact. He hit in three feet of water and skipped like a rock toward the beach. Dazed and a little relieved that he was still in one piece, he sat up and checked himself to see what damage was done. He looked around and began to quickly assess his situation. The flares illuminated only the broken, sinking stern of what was left of the Mako, and he could see a set of running lights heading for Edisto. He had just a few cuts and scrapes but was in good shape otherwise. He still had his docksiders, fishing outfit, and his rain gear. He still had his boot knife and his pocket survival kit. Looking around the beach, he couldn't see much because of the rain and darkness but was able to locate two life preservers.

The flares were quickly fading. *Best make the most of what light I have*, he thought. He stood and jogged over to the little stream that ran from the interior of the island. He tasted the fresh water and began to wade upstream. The rain continued to come down, and he couldn't see but a few feet in front as he trudged ahead. He wadded up onto a dry sandbar and decided to make the best of it. The rain began to slacken, and the clouds began to break from the west. The almost-full moon began to illuminate his surroundings. He found an old tree top further up the bar and drug it away from the bank. He shook it in hopes that any nighttime residents might be persuaded to vacate his newfound shelter. He threw his Stearns raincoat over the side of a branch to break the wind and lay the pants on the sandbar. He sat down and assessed the situation. How could he salvage what was left of the operation?

He had pinpointed the location of a strong radioactive source and made a waypoint on his GPS that was still attached by the lanyard to his belt. He needed to get away from Edisto and bring something from Beaufort to retrieve the object. Getting off the Island would be the first challenge and then the rest might be easier. He relaxed and tried to rest but was again dealing with the burning hatred in his head.

He thought about his Dad he never met. He hated never having a father. All of the other kids had fathers and if you lived on an Air Force base you needed a father. You needed someone to guide you through the trials and tribulations of growing up in a military man's world. You needed a father so you could be like everyone else.

Chapter 57

The Big Drop

On August 6, 1945, Robert W. Savage Sr. was in a Japanese prisoner-of-war camp. He was captured when his B-29 was shot down in a raid over Tokyo. He and the plane's navigator managed to stay together during their ordeal and had been taken to prisoner camp number forty-four. It was located just outside of Hiroshima, and there were only ten other prisoners interned there. Although he had only been there for three weeks, he still liked to hear the droning sounds of the American bombers that came over almost daily to bomb Japan. But they always seemed to go right on by toward the north to bomb other cities. Still, he liked knowing that the Japanese were finally paying the price for attacking Pearl Harbor.

This day, there was a faint sound that he and his fellow prisoners could barely hear. It sounded like a small group of two or three bombers at very high altitude. They each guessed what it could mean, another drop of leaflets or another reconnaissance mission? Then, suddenly, as they were looking up, trying to spot the vapor trails, there was a bright flash of light. And all that was left of the three men standing in the open were their shadows. The first nuclear bomb used in war vaporized them completely.

Captain Mikell hated the country that would kill its own servicemen. And they would pay, and he would get paid—maybe not today but someday.

Chapter 58

Back at the Dock

Bekka couldn't make much speed, even though she pushed hard to catch the other boat. Apparently, she had damaged the lower unit of the port motor on the Contender and could not get up on plane, even with the controls pushed hard to full. She would have to be satisfied that she had destroyed one drug dealer's boat. As her target turned into Big Bay Creek, she turned up St. Pierre Creek to cut across to her boat house.

Springer pulled alongside the Edisto Seafood dock; everyone was there. Bo threw a blanket around Maggy, and Hubby grabbed the line and handed Springer the half-empty beer he had been drinking. He looked at Hubby and then at the beer. He threw it in a crab box as he hurried past. They all moved quickly into the seafood house. Maggy crying, grabbed Springer, and wouldn't let go. Ashley and Barry tied up the Whaler and ran in to get out of the rain that was coming down even harder now. Warren stood behind everyone and just listened.

"He tried to run me down with the Mako!" she cried. "He was going to kill me! Why? What did I do?"

The detective tried to calm her down. "It's OK. You're safe now. What happened to him?"

Springer responded, "Another boat was out there, jumped over the sandbar, and landed across the Mako. I saw his bow fly up in the air with him in it. I don't think he could have survived that crash."

"Who was the other boat?" Bo asked.

"Don't know; never got a good look at it. I got Maggy and got the hell out of there as fast as we could run without lights."

She snuggled up against him even tighter and almost knocked him off the bench. "You saved my life. You could have gotten killed too, you know? He had a shotgun."

"Yeah, I know, but I couldn't leave you. I could never leave you."

She looked into his eyes as if seeing someone new for the first time. They had grown up together and picked on one another their entire lives, but this was the first time she realized that she loved him and had always loved him. She grabbed his strong arms, put them around her, and whispered to him, "Please! Never let go of me!"

He had always been in love with her and watched over her, even when she didn't know it. "I'll be right here," he said softly.

Bo said they needed a safe place to go. Bobby Fontana called out, "Everyone, to my house. Call the others and tell them to take turns watching the creek and the drive. Somebody has something this guy wants real bad. And we don't know who has it or what it is."

"And he's willing to kill for it," added Ashley.

Bo said, "I've got two more deputies on the way. One will meet you at your house, Bobby, and stay all night; the other one's on his way here. Springer, I need you to gas up and get me and the other deputy over to Otter as soon as you can get that boat ready."

Maggy looked up at him and said in a voice she had never used with her uncle, "No! Springer stays with me." She glared hard as if to make him understand she meant it.

Springer took her arms from around him and said, "It's OK. We just have to go see what's left of that guy and the Mako. Go with Bobby and the boys; someone needs to get Suzy and the girls to Bobby's too. This might be the same fellow who tried to kidnap her."

Moving toward the door, Barry yelled, "We're on it. We'll get them to the house."

Hubby stepped in: "You're all gassed up and ready to go, Capt. Springer. She's idling on the dock!"

Everyone started to head out in their own directions. Maggy grabbed Springer and kissed him like never before. "You damn well better come back to me, James Leroy Springer!"

"I will. I'll let you know what's going on. Listen in on channel sixteen on the VHS radio. You can keep up with everything."

Just as they turned to head for the boat, the Coast Guard Dolphin helicopter flew in low and loud in the dark rainy sky and spun quickly to hover with its powerful searchlights on the Boston Whaler.

He looked back and yelled to her, "Calvary has arrived!"

The second deputy ran onto the dock with body armor and rifles and disappeared down the ramp and onto the Whaler.

She yelled back, "Don't you be a hero, Jamie Springer. Once a day is enough!"

Chapter 59

Capt. Gets Away

Capt. Mikell knew they would come looking for him on Otter Island soon, and they would surely call in the Coast Guard with their thermal search equipment. He had to move away quickly and get to a more secure spot. And he had to cover his heat signature. The tide was still going out, but it was about to change. If he could get to the southern end of the island and float out with the tide, then he could let the northeast wind push him back inshore where the current would take him to Hunting Island. There, he could steal a vehicle in the state park and regroup. He grabbed the life jackets for cover and quickly started walking south.

Chapter 60

Deep Water

A bonnethead shark cruised over the sixty-foot-deep scour hole on Fishing Creek at the end of Otter Island. It had become a favorite spot for sharks because dead fish and crabs would fall in with the changing tides. And the big metal casing at the bottom had a steady, warm glow that also attracted lots of fish.

Chapter 61

Life Goes On

It had been two over two weeks since that night on Otter Island.

The only excitement was when the employees at Whaley's restaurant caught the manager, Lowell, outside after drinking too much and wrapped him to the telephone pole with plastic wrap until he promised everyone a raise.

But on this cloudy Sunday afternoon, everyone came to Whaley's for an impromptu memorial service—for Cecil, who still had parts missing; for Mr. Beal, who everyone knew as a good guy who must have gotten caught up in something bad; and, again, for Freedia, Bo's wife. Wayland Clampet, the Episcopal padre, presided. Fourteen-year-old Brantley Patrick helped with the communion. And, as always, little Brantley drank what was left of the communion wine (in the chalice and the bottle.)

Sweet William was found at Prospect Hill by a couple of teens looking for a romantic spot. They arrived by boat right after Capt.

Mikell drove off to head for Otter Island. They first thought someone was trying to play Dr. Frankenstein with all of the medical equipment and white curtains. But when they saw who it was, they realized that William had been kidnapped or he and his friends were playing freaky again. Anyway, he was free and no worse for wear. He had been checked out at St. Francis Hospital and questioned by what seemed like every policeman in the county.

Detective McKee had a copy of Capt. Mikell's Vermont driver's license, a few finger prints, and that was it. None of it matched any database he could find. They found no body, no parts of a body, nothing to go on. The sheriff wasn't happy, and Bo heard about it every day.

The Department of Energy, Homeland Security, Coast Guard, and the Federal Immigration and Customs Enforcement Department arrived with a battalion of scientists and investigators. No one was sure why the immigration guys were there. Maybe they thought there were aliens involved. They looked high and low for the bomb and found nothing. They still said it had to be closer to Tybee Island, Georgia. But then they really had no idea where the thing was. But all the hubbub had been good for the local economy in the offseason.

Maggy and Jamie Springer were inseparable. Her eyes had been opened to a world she never knew yet lived every day. She felt so ashamed for not realizing who really loved her. She wouldn't make that mistake again. The wedding would be next spring.

Denique stood at the front door of the dilapidated old house. The bright red hand was flashing erratically and buzzing. The words "Palm Reader" in green faded in and out. Her friend Elly stood behind her just within arm's reach. She gave her a quick shove. "Go ahead. Ring the bell!" she whispered real low.

"I can't," said the trembling voice of the frightened young woman.

"Don't you want to know what really happened to Beal? Miss Pearl is the only way you'll find the truth," she whispered again and nodded affirmatively as she backed up slowly.

The door opened with a creek and a groan. A pale, thin white hand motioned for her to come in…

But now Warren had been missing for the past two weeks. So where was he, and what could he have gotten himself into?

The end!

Reference

*https://en.wikipedia.org/wiki/1958_Tybee_Island_mid-air_collision